BEAUTY

Also available from

SARAH PINBOROUGH & TITAN BOOKS

Poison
Charm

BEAUTY

A WICKED *SLEEPING BEAUTY* TALE

SARAH PINBOROUGH

TITAN BOOKS

Beauty
Print edition ISBN: 9781783291144
E-book edition ISBN: 9781783291168

Published by Titan Books
A division of Titan Publishing Group Ltd
144 Southwark Street, London SE1 0UP

First edition: May 2015
2 4 6 8 10 9 7 5 3 1

A CIP catalogue record for this title is available from the British Library.

Printed and bound in Spain.

FOR LOU & JOE ABERCROMBIE

Great friends and great people. With love.

BEAUTY

1

'He needs an adventure...'

It was a warm spring and the king and queen took their breakfast on the balcony outside their private apartments, enjoying the fresh air without the burden of any sort of protocol. The sun was warm without burning and the sky was bright with out making them squint. For the queen it was almost perfect. The only thing spoiling the moment was the subject of their conversation. It was, however, a talk they both knew was overdue.

'He needs to grow up,' she said, sipping her tea. 'We've spoiled him, I fear.'

'It's very hard not to spoil a prince,' her husband, the king replied gruffly. 'No doubt my father spoiled me. A prince must feel superior. How else can they ever become a good king?'

The king's stomach was bursting free of his thick white dressing gown and as he reached for another pastry the queen marvelled at how time changed them all. The handsome young prince she'd married had disappeared, swallowed up by this bear of a man. It had been a good marriage though, difficult as she found the endless pressures of royalty, and in the main he had been a good husband as well as a good king.

'Still,' she added. 'He's our only child. I think perhaps we've been too soft on him.'

'Perhaps you're right,' he grunted. 'He must soon marry and start a family of his own. He should attend more council meetings. Undertake more training with the generals for when he must lead the army. Learn to understand the revenue as he promised to.' He paused and frowned. 'What does he do with his time anyway?'

The conversation wouldn't have started if they hadn't seen their only child, the hope of the kingdom, their handsome golden boy, staggering up the castle steps in a wine soaked shirt as they'd taken their seats on the balcony that morning. It had become something of a habit, as a quick chat with the servants had revealed. Being out all night at inns and houses of ill repute with various other young men of noble birth, then sleeping most of the day away. Occasionally riding out with the hunt, but too often not.

It was all, perhaps, to be expected of a young man, but it was becoming a lifestyle and that would not do. Their boy was going to be a king one day, and that would require a level of gravitas and respect that he currently did not have. The queen looked at her husband again. He was no longer a fit ox of a man. His face was red and veins had burst on his cheeks. He was carrying far too much weight. Her son's destiny might be closer to hand than any of them liked to think – and although no parent liked to think it of their own flesh and blood, the queen had become concerned of late that her boy would not rise to the challenge.

'We need to find him a good woman,' she said. 'Someone with a calm temperament and a clever brain.' It was easier to consider the qualities of a future wife than to discuss the flaws in the prince.

'He'll want a pretty wife,' the king muttered and then smiled at his queen. 'I was lucky. I found that truly rare creature: a woman with both beauty and brains.'

The queen said nothing but shared a contented moment with him, knowing that the king too felt they had spent their years together well. Yes, she suffered from terrible headaches and various forms of anxiety, but she had been a good advisor to him behind the closed doors of their rooms and when he'd strayed, as kings, the most spoiled of all men, were wont to do, she had shrugged it away and known that he would be back in her bed before long. It was a royal marriage after all, and she'd had romance before it, a long time ago. Romance and—

'He needs an adventure,' she said, the words out before she'd really thought it through. 'All these wild nights; they're not good for him. He needs a proper adventure.'

'Hmmm,' the king said. 'The thought had occurred to me. But to send him from the kingdom? Our only son?'

'A king needs to know the outside world,' the queen said. 'He needs to understand how the nine kingdoms are different. Why they are at war. Perhaps find a way to make peace with an enemy. He can't do any of that here.'

The king knew the wisdom of his wife's words and somewhere in the recesses of his mind a memory stirred. 'My grandfather had such adventures, you know. When I was a child he told stories of visiting a faraway land and rescuing a girl from a tower by climbing her hair.'

They both laughed at that and the queen's eyes twinkled. 'I hope he was a slim man at the time.'

'I'd break your neck before I'd got one foot on the wall, wouldn't I?' The king shook his head. 'A crazy story from a crazy old man. But still, I think there is something to this adventure idea.'

The queen watched as her husband slipped off into his own thoughts. His eyes were narrowed and she knew better than to speak and interrupt him. Her seed was sown and now he'd be trying to determine the best kind of adventure for their son to have. One that was important enough, not too dangerous, but which might benefit the kingdom. After all, the kingdom was the only thing that mattered when every thing was said and done.

She sipped her tea and leaned back in her chair, gazing up at the turrets far above her and the many, many windows that glinted brightly in the sunshine. Her head was mercifully free of pain and today there were no official engagements or lunches with noble women for her to attend. Birds sang in the trees. Below them the city rumbled into life. She felt content with her lot.

'I think I have it,' her husband said eventually. 'I think I have the very thing.'

The king spoke to his son about it over dinner. Being a relatively wise king he invited several influential noblemen to dine with them, along with their sons. A prince was as likely to bow to peer pressure as any other young man, and now that the king and queen had made their decision he would brook no arguments from his son about the task he was about to set him.

'Plague?' the prince said after his father had started speaking. 'What kind of plague?'

'I don't know,' the king answered. 'It might just be a legend. All anyone knows is that deep in the heart of the forest, near the base of the Far Mountain, there was once a wealthy city. A tenth kingdom. The story goes that nearly a hundred years ago a terrible plague struck the city. The forest, rich with magic so close to the mountain's edge, closed in around it, the trees and brambles growing so high and thick that the city and all its people were sealed off and lost forever.'

'And no one looked for them?' the prince asked.

His venison sat untouched on his plate and the king was pleased to see the story had his son's attention. But then the boy had always chosen romanticism over practicality.

'Perhaps they did, but the forest didn't allow them to be found.'

'Surely they could have cut themselves free from the other side?'

'But they didn't. Which leads me to believe that the entire population died very quickly.' The king paused. 'But of course, all the treasures will still be there. And if the city could be found, it would make a welcome addition to our kingdom. A lucrative discovery, a useful outpost for keeping an eye on our enemies or a perfect place to host peace talks between warring kings.'

'And you want to find it?' the prince asked.

The king smiled and sipped his wine. 'No, my son. I want *you* to find it. Every prince should go out into the world and have an adventure before settling down. This will be yours.'

Several of the young men around the table burst into excited chatter and the prince, the jewel at their centre, grinned. 'Then I shall find it for you, father! I promise you I shall!'

The huntsman had been lost in the dream when his father woke him. It was the same dream he'd had for several nights and it was so powerful that the echo of it stayed with him during the days. There was a girl with hair that tumbled in thick curls down her back, as red as autumn leaves. She was running through the forest and he was chasing her, following the flashes of her hair and the echo of her laughter, but all the time her face was out of sight. He ran as he had as a child, with no sense of awareness of the changing shape of the forest around him and without the tracking skills that had become second nature to him as a man. Nature didn't matter. The beasts that lived around him didn't matter. The forest itself, so much a part of him, no longer mattered in his dream. All he cared about was finding the girl who stayed so elusive ahead of him. His breath rushed in his ears and his heart raced.

He sat up with a start, for a moment confused by his surroundings. His father grinned at him. 'The girl again?'

He nodded.

'I told you. She's your true love. You're lucky; not many get the dreams. But if you do, you have to find her.'

'Well, she's not in the village, that's for sure.' The

huntsman stretched and yawned.

'And a good thing too. You've had most of the girls here. Or they've had you.'

They smiled at each other, good natured, easy with the natural way of men and women, and how frequently they tumbled into bed with each other until wedding vows claimed them. Men and women both were just animals after all, and life in the forest could be hard. Comforts had to be taken where you could get them.

'Why did you wake me?' The huntsman, said as he shook away his sleepiness and pulled on his shirt. Beyond the glow of his father's torch, he could tell it was still dark outside and the air held the crisp scent of a chill spring night. It wasn't dawn, but maybe two or three in the morning.

'The king's men want you.' His father held up a hand. 'It's nothing bad. They want the best young huntsman and the elders have all chosen you.'

'I *am* the best,' the huntsman muttered. 'But what do they want me to hunt?'

He peered out the window and saw several soldiers in shining uniforms, sitting high on thoroughbred horses.

'They want you to babysit the prince. Be his companion on a trip to the edge of the Far Mountain.'

The huntsman's heart fell. He had no time for kings or princes. From what he'd heard around the campfires on the long winter hunts, nothing good ever came from their company. 'Can't he take care of himself?' he asked.

His father snorted with laughter. 'He's a prince. He's no match for the forest. He'll be lost within a day. Starving within two—'

'—and eaten within three,' the huntsman finished.

The horses outside pawed at the ground, picking up on their riders' impatience.

'I don't have a choice, do I?' he said, reaching for his knife and his axe and his old leather bag for carrying food and water.

'No, son, you don't. The king's decided his boy needs an adventure.' His father's tanned, wrinkled face looked like a craggy rock face in the gloomy light. 'But maybe you do too.' He smiled. 'Maybe you'll find that redhead of yours out there.'

'The girl of my dreams?' the huntsman said, wryly.

'Stranger things have happened.'

'If this prince doesn't get me killed first,' he said and stepped out into the night. He didn't look back at his father, or at any of the huntsmen and women who had gathered in front of their small cottages and huts to watch him leave. Long farewells weren't their way. He'd either come home or he wouldn't. Huntsmen knew each other well enough to know the things that were so often said by other men – and to know how rarely they were meant. He climbed up on the back of a waiting horse and patted its neck. The beast whinnied as nature recognised nature, and then they were gone, leaving the village behind in the pale pre-dawn light.

* * *

The huntsman had been to the city before but had only visited the markets on its edges. The castle at its heart glittered like a diamond when the sun hit the banks of sparkling windows, but it had always seemed like an illusion in the distance. It was beyond him how men could build such edifices and he wondered how many ordinary people had died cutting, dragging and lifting the thousands of quarried stones that made up its smooth, perfect surface. He wondered if the king ever wondered that.

Now that he was standing in front of the man, he doubted it. Gruff and ageing as the king was, he had sharp, cool eyes within his fattening face.

'They say you're the best of the huntsmen,' the king said as he studied the man before him. 'That no one knows the forest as well as you.'

'I know the forest, that's true,' the huntsman answered. He had no intention of expounding upon his own skills. The king had already formed his opinion, otherwise they wouldn't be face to face. Boasting just set a man up for a fall, and the only reason to boast would be to somehow ingratiate himself with the king for personal favour or political gain. The huntsman wanted nothing from the king for, unlike so many, the glittering life did not appeal to him. He neither understood nor trusted it.

'And you're good with a knife? And a bow?'

The huntsman shrugged. 'I'm a huntsman. Those are my tools.'

'You don't say much,' the king said, smiling as he leaned back in his vast, ornate throne, inlaid with rubies and emeralds so large that the huntsman could almost see his reflection in them. 'I like that.' He waited for a moment as if expecting the huntsman to respond to his praise, and then his smile fell to seriousness and he continued. 'The prince is my only son. He needs an adventure. He also needs to come back alive. He is my heir and the kingdom needs him.'

'I'll do my best,' the huntsman said. 'But I am only one man.'

'If you were to return without him, it would not end well for you.' Any pretence at warmth had vanished from the king's face. 'Or for your village.'

His father, not without an adventure or two of his own below his belt, had warned him about the merciless ways of the rich and royal, and the king's threat came as no surprise. 'As I said: I'll do my best, your majesty. My best is all I have to offer.'

The king frowned for a moment as he tried to work out whether the huntsman was being ignorant, obtuse or just speaking plainly in a place where every sentence was normally laden with subtext, but eventually nodded and grunted.

'Good.' He ran thick fingers over his ruddy cheek. 'The prince must never know about this conversation. He knows you are to be his guide, and that your skills will be needed to pass through the forest, but he must believe that he's the hero in this tale, do you understand? Your role in protecting him must never be spoken of.'

The huntsman nodded. He had no time for heroes or stories or tales of true love, despite his own dreams.

'Good,' the king said again. 'Good.'

The huntsman met the prince down by the stables where he was choosing their horses, fine steeds whose muscles rippled under their glossy dark hides. The prince was as blond as the huntsman was dark and his easy smile charmed all those around him. At least he looked fit, the huntsman thought, and they were of a similar age. Perhaps it wouldn't be such a bad journey. The prince shook his hand vigorously and then pulled him close, patting the huntsman heartily on the back.

'We leave at first light,' he said and then winked. 'Which gives us all night in the taverns to give this city – and its maidens – our farewells! There will be wine and women for us, my new friend, before we leave to find a new castle for the kingdom!'

The huntsman forced a smile as his heart sank. He had no problem with wine and women – especially not with the women – but it appeared the prince was in danger of believing the legends of his princely deeds even before he had done any. That was never good. When huntsmen got too cocky they normally ended up gored. What would happen to this fine, handsome prince, he wondered. And how on earth was he going to save him from it?

2

'Bloody bastard wolves...'

She hadn't meant to come back this way but when her feet had turned her down the path she had followed them. Her basket was full and heavy and she should have gone straight to granny's cottage, but the forest came alive in the spring and nowhere were the scents more alive than at the edge of the impenetrable wall of briars and bushes and, as usual, she couldn't resist their lure.

None of the villagers ever came here. They spoke in whispers about it and the noises that could sometimes be heard in the night, and children stayed away, but Petra had always been drawn to it. She placed her basket on the rich long grass and pushed back the hood of her red cape so that she could gaze upwards. The dark green wall stretched up as high as she could see, blocking out any sight of the mountain, coloured here and there by small bursts of flowers poking through the brambles.

As she did every time, she wrapped her hands in her cloak to protect her from hidden thorns and tried to pull a few branches apart to see what lay on the other side, but it was a fruitless task and all she could make out were more twigs and vines, all locking together. She held her breath and listened, but there was only birdsong and the rustle of the forest. That was *all* there ever was in the daylight and she couldn't fight the disappointment she felt. Perhaps she'd sneak out again tonight and see if she could hear the plaintive howling that sometimes carried quietly over the briar wall on the breeze. The sound might have terrified men and children alike, but something in it called to Petra and made her heart ache. For a while she had just listened, but then one night she'd thrown her hood back and howled in response and the forest wall itself had trembled as their two voices became one. It had become a song between them, a delicious, private secret that made her shiver in ways she didn't really understand. But she longed to see beyond the wall and find the other half of her duet. What manner of beast was trapped there? Why did it sound so lonely? And what had made the forest create such a daunting, impenetrable fortress that no man had tried to break through it?

'I thought I'd find you here.'

Petra jumped slightly at the soft voice and turned. 'Sorry, granny. I just...'

'I know,' her grandmother said. 'You just wandered here by accident.' She was a short, stout woman whose face was rosy with both good humour and good nature. Here and there a grey curl sprung out from under her cap. Petra loved her very, very much. 'The forest can be like that with places and people. When your mother, may she rest in peace, was little she was always up at the emerald pond. She'd stare into it for hours, hoping to see a water witch or some such foolishness.' She smiled and Petra smiled back, picking up her basket and turning her back on the lush vegetation that grew so unnaturally and fascinated her. She'd heard her mother's story many times before but she never tired of it and she knew it cheered her grandmother, although by nature a happy soul, to talk about her.

'I've put some soup on for lunch,' her granny said. 'Let's go home.'

They chatted about their mornings as they walked, the route second nature to them both even though the tiny paths that cut through the dense woodland would barely be noticeable to a stranger. The stream somewhere to their left finally joined them, babbling into their conversation as they walked alongside the flowing water, and finally came to the clearing where granny's cottage sat. Smoke rose from the chimney and flowers were starting to bloom in the borders that ran in front of the small house. It should have been a beautiful sight but today, as had happened on too many days recently, it was marred by a bloody trail of innards that emerged from behind the house and vanished at the edge of the forest.

'Oh, not again!' Granny gasped and the two women, age being no impediment to panic, ran to the small enclosure behind the cottage where granny kept her precious goats. It was as Petra feared. The gate had been broken through yet again. From somewhere deep in the trees a low howl of victory drifted towards them. It had none of the plaintive texture of the sound that drew Petra to the mysterious forest wall; this was all animal, fierce and hungry.

'Bloody wolves,' her granny swore. 'Bloody bastard wolves.'

'I'll mend it again,' she said, quietly. 'Make it stronger.'

Her grandmother was moving through the rest of the scared goats who had huddled at the far corner of the pen. 'Adolpho. It's taken Adolpho.'

Petra had never tried to persuade her grandmother to move to one of the houses in the village as she grew older – she knew how much the old lady loved the peace and quiet of the forest – but recently she'd started to think it might be a good idea. It had been a hard winter and the wolves, normally a rarity in this part of the forest, had arrived as a hungry pack and, when the weather broke, they'd stayed. Where foxes were a menace they'd learned to deal with, the winter wolves were braver and stronger. Men in the village talked of cattle lost in the night to the wolves working in twos and threes, and although they had tried to hunt them, the pack was elusive.

'Go inside, Granny,' Petra said, knowing that the old woman would want a quiet moment to mourn the loss of the animal. 'I'll clean up out here.' The wolves would be back, that she knew for certain, and she couldn't help but wonder how long it would be before they saw the stout old woman as an easy meal. Especially if they couldn't get to the goats. She needed a fence as high as that wall of greenery around her granny's cottage. She needed to protect her. The wolf's gruff howl was joined by another and she was sure they were mocking her. She cursed them silently, then went to the shed and pulled out more planks of wood and rolls of wire. She would not give up. The wolves would not win. Her hair fell into her eyes as she worked, angrily focused on her task and wishing that the wolf from far away would come and scare these rough relatives away for her. At least then her fingers wouldn't be full of splinters and her skin slick with sweat.

She was halfway through the job when there was a crash from inside the cottage, a scream, and the sound of plates being dropped.

'Granny!' Her heart in her mouth, she turned and ran.

They had been travelling through the forest for several days before the two men eased into a comfortable silence. The first day, once out of sight of the fanfare and grand send off the king had arranged for his son, had been a relatively slow one given the prince's hangover. The huntsman's own head was clear having been on the outskirts of the group for the night, gritting his teeth every time the prince introduced him to some new dandy as his servant. Huntsmen served no one but nature. He'd drunk one or two cups of beer but the group of rowdy young men hadn't impressed him and neither had they particularly encouraged him to join them, which suited him just fine. He was glad when dawn broke and he could wake the prince and prepare to get out of the city. He'd had enough. He wanted their 'adventure' over so he could return to his people, and at least in the forest he would feel that he was almost home.

By the time they'd made camp, the fresh air had revived the prince's spirits enough for him to make a fire while the huntsman fetched water and killed a rabbit for their dinner. At first the prince had been determined to prove his superiority by trying to impress the huntsman with tales of castle living, but after a while he'd become curious about his companion's way of life. The huntsman answered his questions as best he could as he skinned and cooked the animal, and it was clear that the prince, away from the peer pressure of his cohort, was begrudgingly beginning to admire his companion. The huntsman relaxed his own judgement on the royal in return.

The next few days passed well and they even laughed together occasionally at some joke or story one or other would tell. They might not have been a natural pairing for a friendship, but it wasn't the prince's fault that the king had dragged the huntsman from his home and rested this burden – and the fate of his village – on his shoulders. He would make the best of it and perhaps they would both come out of the experience better and wiser men.

After ten days of travelling the Far Mountain had grown taller in the skyline and the forest thicker; green and lush and rich with life. The light scent of spring in the air became tinged with something heavier, and when they finally found a large pond to drink from the water was bitter and they had to spit it out. The prince declared it was magic they could taste and shuddered slightly, afraid. The huntsman pointed out that magic was simply nature in another guise and nothing to be either feared or courted, but before they could get into an argument about it he saw chimney smoke drifting up from behind some trees to their right.

'They'll know where there's good water,' the huntsman said.

'Isn't it your job to find it?' the prince shot back.

The huntsman ignored him and found an almost invisible path through the trees that led to a small clearing at the heart of which sat a cottage surrounded by pretty flowers... and by the faintest blood stained trail through the grass that none other than an animal or a huntsman would be likely to spot. He frowned slightly; there had been trouble here. He paused and looked up. The door was open and from inside came the crashing of plates and a short scream. He gripped the hilt of his knife and ran forward.

'Granny!' A girl's shout came from somewhere behind the cottage but the huntsman and the prince didn't pause. They ran straight inside.

A low growl came from beyond the cosy main room and the two men knocked over a side table as they followed it, the prince with his sword drawn and the huntsman with his knife.

A large grey wolf, teeth bared, was scrabbling and scratching at a tall cupboard door in the corner. It suddenly jerked open an inch and a broom handle poked out sharply and jabbed at the beast. 'Shoo! Shoo!'

The prince, clearly nervous, was waving his sword so high in the small room that the huntsman had to duck to avoid losing an ear.

'Watch what you're doing with that thing,' he muttered, as the wolf turned to face them. It snarled, ready to pounce. Faced with the full sight of its bloody mouth and sharp teeth, the prince paled. 'Perhaps we should run.'

'We can't outrun it,' the huntsman said, his voice low. The wolf growled again, and the prince trembled slightly, grabbing at the huntsman's arm and tugging him backwards – and off balance – ruining any chance he had of defending them.

Sensing their fear, the wolf leapt, across the table at them, all raging heat and hunger. The huntsman shoved the clinging prince away, sending him flying into a dresser and breaking more crockery, but as the beast loomed over him his own balance was gone and he cursed under his breath, preparing to feel the sharp thick claws and heavy teeth tearing into his skin.

An arrow whistled past him, straight and true, and struck firmly lodging several inches deep in the wolf's chest. All momentum suddenly lost, it mewled and dropped, crashing onto the table. It shuddered for a second and then was gone. As the prince got to his feet, the huntsman stared at the dead beast, and then turned to look behind him at the girl holding the bow.

'You can come out now, Granny,' she said, softly. 'It's dead.'

The girl stared at the wolf with a mixture of loathing and sadness and then turned her eyes to the men; one dressed in the finest clothes with royal insignia on his red cloak and sword, and the other in the rough green fabrics and tan leathers of a working huntsman.

'Can I help you?' she asked.

'We heard the scream,' the huntsman said. 'And came to help. But it seems you had it all under control.'

'We were hoping you could direct us to the nearest

stream,' the prince said, as if he hadn't been trembling in fear only seconds before and there was no dead wolf bleeding over the kitchen table. 'We've been travelling for days and this part of the forest is strange to us. We found a pond, but the water was undrinkable. And then we heard the crash and saw the door was open, and came inside.'

'Oh, they say that pond's cursed. But that can wait until we've had our somewhat late lunch. The wolves have ruined our day.'

A small, stout woman with a cheerful face lent character by a life in the forest, stepped out of the cupboard, put the broom she was holding away, and then smiled at them. 'You will be staying for some food, I presume? The stew's nearly done and there's plenty to go round.'

The girl sighed and put her hands on her hips. 'We don't know them, granny. They could be anyone.'

Her grandmother peered over her glasses and looked the men up and down.

'Everyone's someone, Petra dear, and that one has the manners of royalty about him, and the other looks like a huntsman to me. You can always trust a huntsman, that's what my mother told me. Now, come on, having visitors will be nice.' She smiled warmly. 'I'm always curious when strangers from distant places turn up at my door, and so should you be.'

'They can help me clear up first then.' The girl didn't

look as convinced as her grandmother.

'We'll be more than happy to help,' the prince said, and gave the girl a curt bow. She didn't look too impressed, but instead grabbed the wolf's forelegs. 'Then one of you give me a hand getting this outside.'

As Petra and her granny cleaned the cottage, the huntsman and the prince worked hard to make the goat pen secure. When they were done, the huntsman smeared the wolf's blood on all the posts until they looked almost painted red. The goats shuffled nervously inside.

'It'll help keep the wolves away,' he said, as Petra came and inspected their work. 'And better the goats are nervous than dead.' She didn't disagree, and he saw a little of the tension escaping her shoulders. They might not be friends yet, but perhaps they were no longer irritating strangers.

The cottage was warm and cosy and it was good to spend a night inside. Petra fetched them some wine and there was bread and stew enough for them all to be full and have some left over. The huntsman was pleased when he saw the young prince leave a few gold coins on the dresser when he thought no one was looking. By the time they'd eaten night had fallen and they sat gathered round the comforting warmth and light of the large fire in the grate.

'So,' Granny said, her knitting needles clicking together

and her chair rocking slightly under her. 'What brings you to this corner of the kingdoms?'

'We're in search of a legend,' the prince said. 'My father has sent me to find a lost castle, vanished for nearly a hundred years. Apparently it's hidden behind a forest wall of some kind—'

'A wall of forest?' Petra sat upright in her chair. 'I know where—'

'Shhh dear,' her granny patted her knee. 'All in good time.'

It was the most animated the girl had been since their arrival, and that intrigued the huntsman. Unlike the city girls she seemed unimpressed by the handsome prince, and he liked her all the more for that.

'Why does your father send you to find it?' the old lady asked.

'He thinks all young men should have an adventure,' the huntsman cut in, before the prince could muddy the waters of their travel with talk of outposts and amassing land.

'And that's a good enough reason,' Granny said and she smiled, nodded and put down her knitting.

'Have you heard of this place?' the prince asked.

'Oh yes.' Granny's eyes twinkled. 'My mother would speak of it sometimes. Mainly when she was older than I am now, and her mind was not always as it should have been. It sounded a strange place, from her tales. But then most cities are strange and, to be fair, she was always full of fancy stories which no one knew the truth of.'

'I go to the wall,' Petra said suddenly. Her face was flushed and alive. 'Sometimes I hear a sound from the other side. A lonely, echoing cry. It haunts me.'

'I think it's more than that, dear,' her grandmother's eyes twinkled fondly as she looked at her. 'You should go with them.'

'Oh no,' Petra said, holding her granny's arm. 'I'll stay here with you. I need to keep you safe.'

'Don't be silly, dear. It's not just men who need adventures, you know. Everyone has their own destiny to find. And if there's something over that wall that's calling to you, you have to find it. That's the way of things.'

'No,' Petra said, although it was clear in her eyes that she was desperate to go. 'There are still too many wolves in the forest. If the pen holds and they can't get to the goats, what if they come for you again? Like today?'

The huntsman looked thoughtfully at the two women and then left them by the fire with the prince and went outside. He dragged the wolf's body into the forest to work on it and then took the result to the pond to wash it clean, relying on his forest instincts to lead him where he needed to go. By the time he was done he was sweating but pleased.

'Here,' he said, and held up his completed work. 'This will keep them away. They'll smell one of their own instead of you.'

'What *is* that?' Petra asked.

'A wolf wrap,' the huntsman said. He helped the old lady put the wolf's skin on, and then wrapped her own blanket round her shoulders and placed her cap back on top.

'It's lovely and cosy,' she said from somewhere under the wolf's snout. Her hands, under the wolf's claws, looked strange as she continued her knitting.

'You look so peculiar,' Petra giggled. 'Like a wolf has dressed up in your clothes!' They all laughed aloud as the old lady rocked her chair backwards and forwards. 'Well, I quite like it,' she said. 'I can save on wood for the fire if I have this keeping me toasty. And you,' she turned to her granddaughter and lifted her head so her own face was visible beneath the wolf's, 'Can now go on your adventure.'

And so it was decided. They would leave their horses in Granny's care and Petra would join them.

The next morning they ate a hearty breakfast of eggs and bacon and forest mushrooms, and Petra's granny packed some bread and cheese for them which she loaded up in the huntsman's knapsack, before fixing Petra's red cloak over her shoulders. She smiled and her eyes twinkled but the girl looked as if she was about to burst into tears.

'I love you, Granny,' she said.

'I love you too, Petra.' She squeezed the girl tight. 'But your life is out there, not here with me. And I shall be just fine.'

She waved them off from the doorway, and then the girl led them towards the forest wall and whatever lay beyond it.

3

'Once upon a time...'

*O*nce upon a time a young king was out hunting in the forest that lay at the edge of his city. He had not long come to the throne, but he was a good man and was mourning the loss of his father rather than relishing his new power and preferred to hunt alone as it gave him some private time away from the rigours of court life and kingship.

It was a warm day and, with his enthusiasm to chase and kill a living creature dampened by his recent loss, he dismounted and walked his horse to a large pond of sparkling blue water that was so cold and deep that it must have been home to a natural spring beneath its bed.

The young king sat by the pool as his mount drank and stared into the surface of the water, lost in his own *thoughts. Now it is said that deep in the heart of the pond that rarest of creatures, a water witch, sensed the young king's distress and looked up. She saw his handsome face, so weighed down with grief and responsibility, and it touched something inside her. She immediately came to the surface, unable to stop herself.*

The young king and the young water witch fell almost instantly in love and in order to be wed she sacrificed her watery home and went back to the city to become his queen.

At first the king's advisors and, indeed, many of the ordinary people, had reservations about their match, but the new queen kept her magic locked away inside her and she was always so kind and ethereal that soon, despite her icy beauty and eyes that changed colour as water does when the sun hits it, they grew to love her almost as much as the king himself did and the kingdom was content.

For the queen's part, sometimes the wild call of the water and the pull of her old solitary life tugged at her, but she hid that longing away with her magic because in the main she was happy and she loved her king so very, very much. Occasionally, when the yearning became too great, she would return and secretly allow her magic a release, diving deep into the water and feeling the cool aching caress on her skin. But the visits were not often, and she never looked back when she walked away from the pool. Her husband was waiting for her, after all.

Only one thing blighted their bliss. The lack of a son or daughter to make their union complete and secure the future of their kingdom. Eventually, as months passed and no sign of a child was to be had, the king, sensing his beautiful wife's growing sadness, asked the advice of a witch who lived in a tower far, far away. He begged her to help them and, after a few minutes' reflection, she smiled and said she would. She told the king that he would be blessed with a daughter. She would be graceful, she would be intelligent and she would be kind. The king smiled and laughed and offered the witch gold and jewels in reward, but she shook her head and raised her hand and said she hadn't finished. There was something more. He should know that the princess would be happy, but one day she would prick herself on a spindle and would sleep for a hundred years. The king was aghast at her words and demanded that it not be so, but the witch disappeared in a cloud of sparkling dust and his words were spoken to an empty room.

Within a year, they learned that the queen was with child. There was much pageantry and the kingdom celebrated. The queen went to the pond to tell the spirits of all the water witches who had lived there before her, whose magic ran in every drop of its clear water, of her great joy, and to ask their advice on how to manage her child, who would no doubt find it hard to be of two such different peoples. The only answer she received was the ripple of the *surface and silence from the spirits. She took that to mean she should not be concerned. She chose to read it that way. She would not allow any concern to spoil her happiness.*

The sun shone on the kingdom and, as she bloomed, everything was perfect. The king, remembering the witch's words, sent his men throughout the kingdom and all the spindles in the land were destroyed. He would keep his child safe. Whatever it took.

Finally, the queen's time arrived. The birth was difficult, and a storm raged over the kingdom, heavy rain flooding the streets. For nearly two days and nights she struggled and sweated and bled and finally, in the wreck of her bed, the tiny healthy baby girl was delivered. The best efforts of all the king's physicians, however, could not save the beautiful queen. She died in her devastated husband's arms. The magical pond in the forest turned bitter over night. In tucked away corners, the king's advisors muttered that they could have predicted this. Happy as they had been, such a union was never meant to be.

Eventually after a month spent locked away in his apartments, the heartbroken king took his baby daughter in his arms, and as she gurgled up at him, pure white streaks in her soft dark hair, he finally spoke.

'Beauty,' he said. 'We shall call her Beauty.'

4

🝰

'A cursed deep sleep...'

After two hours or more of hacking at the thick branches and vines, the tangle of which made up the thick wall, it was clear to all three of the travellers that there was nothing natural about this occurrence. It was also slow, hard work. As the huntsman cut with his axe, the prince and Petra would hold the space he made open and they would all edge forward and beat at the next section. When the branches behind them were released, they would close up again, the splintered wood and severed vines re-linking and entwining so tightly that no break in the join was visible.

They had started the day bantering lightly – especially the prince and Petra, whose excitement was greater than the huntsman's – but soon the only words any of them spoke were purely related to their task. They were all hot and exhausted and crammed together in a tight space that shuffled forwards very slowly, and the huntsman knew that should they stop, or their axes break, the forest would close in around them and they'd be trapped forever.

They tied handkerchiefs over their faces trying to avoid the heady scents that sprang from several of the flowers and seemed determined to lull them to sleep. Even when Petra's slim, firm body was pressed again his own as they moved, the huntsman's body didn't respond. This forest was dangerous and the trees were clearly against them in their work. The huntsman had always trusted the forest. Nature was honest... and nature was very keen to keep them away from whatever lay beyond this wall.

Finally, however, the pig-headedness of men prevailed and they tumbled, gasping and free, from the grip of the wood. The spring sunshine was bright and warm, and they sat on the grass for a moment, laughing and sharing some water and regaining their strength. It was a few seconds before the eerie quiet around them became too much to ignore.

'I can't even hear any birds singing,' Petra said softly as their moods and laughter quietened. 'On a beautiful day like this they should be everywhere.' She frowned up at the empty sky. Ahead of them lay a small city and in the distance, as was the way with all the kingdoms, there sat a castle at its heart.

'It's not just the birds,' the prince said. 'I can't hear anything. No noise at all.'

He was right. Even the trees dotted along the edges of the narrow road didn't rustle as the warm breeze moved through them. The hairs on the back of the huntsman's neck prickled and he kept one hand on the hilt of his hunting knife as they began to walk, once again cursing the king and the prince and the royal necessity for adventures. As if life wasn't adventure enough.

The cart was just over the other side of the slight hill from the forest's edge and Petra gasped when it came into view. The huntsman didn't blame her. It was a strange sight, that was for sure, stopped as it was in the middle of the road with the shire horse laying down in front of it. Around it were a dozen thick wooled sheep with a dog lying in their midst. He wasn't sure what he'd been expecting, but this wasn't it.

As the prince clambered onto the cart, the huntsman crouched and touched the horse. It was warm and blood pumped in a steady rhythm through its body.

'Hey,' the prince said. 'I think he's still alive.' Up on the cart, a fat man's head lolled forward, the reins having slipped from his hands. The prince tried to straighten him up, but the man's weight slid side ways and he lay across the seat. The prince shook him. 'Hey!' he said, loudly, the word a stranger in the eerie silence around them. 'Hey, wake up! Wake up!' The fat man didn't move. He didn't even snore or grunt or shuffle as the prince wobbled him.

The huntsman looked at the animals around him; not one

of them dead and rotten as he'd been expecting to find in this lost kingdom. The prince had struck on it without thinking.

'They're asleep,' he muttered. 'They're all asleep.'

'That can't be right.' Petra dropped to her knees and stroked the sheepdog. 'They can't have been asleep all this time. Not for a hundred years. It isn't possible.'

But it appeared, as they moved on, that it was entirely possible. Every living creature they passed was lost in slumber, apparently having fallen asleep in the same instant. There was a soldiers' outpost as they walked into the first main streets of the city, and two were asleep face down on a chessboard. Others had crumpled in a heap at their sentry posts. The huntsman counted about fifteen. 'That's a lot of soldiers,' he said.

'Maybe they were at war,' the prince answered. 'The kingdoms are always at war.'

It was an apparently affluent city and there were some beautiful mansions set back in their own grounds, again with sleeping soldiers guarding the high gates, but even the ordinary cottages closer to the castle were well maintained, even though the flowerbeds were overgrown with weeds. Here and there long grasses had sprung up everywhere be tween cobbles and flagstones. Animal life might be slumbering but the plant life still grew, although not to the proportions expected. 'Whatever this is, it's affected every living thing,' Petra said, stooping to examine the flowers.

As they moved closer to the centre of the pretty town the huntsman noticed that some houses had the windows roughly boarded up and when he prised the wood from one they saw that the glass behind was smashed and the contents of the house were either broken or ruined in some way. This had clearly been done before the city fell asleep, and he could find no rhyme or reason to the house that had been wrecked. They were ordinary people's homes. What had happened to the people who had lived in them?

After a while they split up to explore more thoroughly, and everything they found was the same. Men, women and children, all asleep in a variety of strange places. One woman's face was badly burned where she'd been making soup on a stove, now a long time cold, and as she slipped to the floor she'd pulled the pan down over her.

Only in one cottage did the huntsman find anyone in their bed. Whoever it was they must have died before whatever happened to send the city to sleep, and all that remained was a skeleton in a nightdress with wisps of thin hair poking out from beneath a black nightcap. A knife stuck through the thin fabric of her dress and now that her flesh had rotted away, it leaned loose against her ribs where some unknown assailant had stabbed it into her breathing body. It was a strange cottage, with none of the bright colours found in so many of the others, and there was a cold, stale dampness hanging in the air as if none of the outside warmth had crept in during the long years that had passed. He looked in the small cupboards and found jars of herbs and bottle of potions with words he didn't understand on the labels. It was a witch's cottage, he was sure. He shivered and was about to leave when the small stove in the tiny main room caught his eye. The door was open a tiny fraction and something glittered inside. He crouched and pulled the black iron door open.

Inside, sitting on a pile of soot, were a pair of sparkling slippers. He reached in and took them out. They were light and warm in his hands. Diamonds, he thought. They were made of diamonds, not glass at all. Why would someone have been trying to burn them? Was this the work of whoever had killed her? Were the two deeds linked in the strange history of this kingdom? He stared at them for several seconds until he heard Petra and the prince calling for him. The woman upstairs was long gone. She would not miss them, and he and his companions might need something to barter with at some point. He slipped the shoes into his bag and got to his feet. If the city were to somehow wake and the shoes were declared missing he would return them. For now, he'd consider them his fee for this babysitting task the king had set him.

'What do you think they are?' the prince asked, as he and Petra climbed the stone steps and examined the lines on the base of the statue more closely. 'These can't be old, can they?'

'No.' The huntsman frowned. Even though it was clear that the whole city was in some kind of a cursed deep sleep, now they were closer to the castle he couldn't shake the feeling that they were being watched. It was an instinct he was trained not to ignore. 'Look at those ones round the other side. That chalk is fresh.' The lines grew more ragged, but they were definitely some form of counting. Were they charting days? Or months? It was hard to tell. There were a lot of them, whichever it was.

'You mean someone's still awake?' Petra asked.

'That can't be right,' the prince said. 'Even if they hadn't fallen asleep, they'd surely be dead by now.'

'Maybe, maybe not,' Petra said cheerily. 'None of this is normal, after all. And I used to hear howling sometimes. Through the wall. Something's alive in here.'

The huntsman wasn't listening to her. A noise, faint and far to his left had caught his attention. Someone was following them. He was sure of it.

'Hello?' he called. 'Anyone there?' There was no answer but a return to silence. 'Come on,' he muttered. 'Let's get to the castle. If there are any answers, we'll find them there.' The prince nodded, not picking up on the huntsman's point. Trouble, when it came to ordinary people, was normally delivered to them by royalty. Whatever had made this city silent, it had started in the castle.

* * *

Petra had never seen anything like it. Even as they'd walked through the city she'd felt slightly overwhelmed by the looming building that rose so high above the ordinary houses she wondered if in the right light it would engulf them all with its shadow, but as they walked through the open gates, carefully stepping over the crumpled heap of soldiers, for the first time in her life she felt small and insignificant. The village, the forest and her grand mother's cottage had been her world, and all the time this whole city had been sleeping so close by. How much more was there that she would never see, even if she spent a lifetime exploring?

'Heavily guarded,' the huntsman said.

Petra glanced at him. His dark eyes scanned the heavily armed men at their feet and she could see the sight bothered him.

'Perhaps they had more to worry about than my father does,' the prince said. 'Who knows what lies on the other side of this kingdom?'

The huntsman nodded but said nothing more. They were a strange pair, this prince and his companion. One so full of charm and courtly grace, the other quiet and hardy. Petra liked them both, but she knew which one she trusted the most. A man of the forest would always win her vote if it came to her own survival. The prince might be good with a sword but she imagined that he'd learned to duel with rules. Killing something living was very different to courtly sword play – the prince had discovered as much in Granny's kitchen when faced by the winter wolf. There were no rules when it came to fighting for your very existence. They were both handsome, though, she'd give them that.

Vines and ivy had crept up the high stone walls, clinging to the mortar between the heavy rocks as if trying to suffocate the life out of the building itself. In the courtyard men and women slept where they'd stood, one still holding a saddle that was no doubt meant for the horse that slept beside him. Another was surrounded by loaves of bread that had tumbled from his basket.

The huntsman pushed a door open and the hinges shrieked, shocked at the movement after so long. The sound echoed as they stepped inside. Dust danced upwards as they moved, suddenly disturbed from its own slumber on the marble floor. Unlike the smaller houses in the city, no passing wind or weather had been able to penetrate the thick wall and Petra felt as if she had truly walked into a forgotten tomb. Her heart thumped as they walked, leaving footprints in the dirt behind them.

'We should split up,' the prince said. His voice was loud and confident. Petra wondered why he didn't find the castle as eerie as she did but then, she supposed, he was used to castles. He was not in awe of the wealth or beauty that lay under the dust of years passed. 'I'll take upstairs. Petra, you stay on this floor.'

'I'll search the lower levels and dungeons,' the huntsman finished. 'But don't touch anyone. If you find anything then shout and wait.'

'Just what I was going to say,' the prince said.

Petra nodded. The idea of searching alone made her shiver but she wasn't going to admit her fear to the two men. If they were happy to do it then she would be too.

'If we can't find the source of this curse by tomorrow,' the huntsman said, 'then we load some riches onto a cart for your father and try and cut our way back out. Agreed?'

The huntsman had barely smiled since they'd found the city. Petra was sure that if it was up to him they'd be leaving it by now. Whatever had brought him here it wasn't thrill-seeking or adventure, but Petra couldn't help feeling a little of those things herself. She couldn't imagine turning her back on this place and not knowing how the story had begun, or how it ended.

'And mark your path on the walls or in the dust,' he said. 'So you can see where you've been and find your way back here.' This time he did give her a small smile and she liked the creases that formed in his cheeks, as if in his normal life he smiled a lot. The instruction was for her alone. The prince might be used to finding his way round castles, but she most definitely wasn't.

* * *

The ground floor of a castle, she'd decided within an hour or so, was a very strange affair. There were three ballrooms; two light and airy and with ceilings painted with beautiful dancing couples, and another further back – which could only be accessed through a library and then a small annexed corridor – that was painted red and decorated with ornate gold and heavy black curtains. It was an odd contrast with the other two and she decided she didn't like it very much at all. The air had a metallic tang to it and, although she was technically trespassing wherever she went, this was the only room in which she felt she'd invaded something secret. No one was sleeping in any of the main function rooms, all of which were breath taking and yet slightly impersonal and as she explored them she decided that royal residences were clearly as much about the visitors as they were about the family that lived there. It was clearly a strange thing to be a royal.

In some kind of meeting room, several grey haired men in sombre robes were asleep on thick documents and open books and more soldiers slept in the doorways. A jug of wine had been knocked across the table and where it had soaked into the polished wood and scattered papers, the stains looked like blood on the large table.

She felt happier when she found the smaller, more ordinary rooms where servants were working. In one long corridor boot boys slept over pots of polish, and in the kitchens the tables were full of half made pies and pastries, the cooks and maids crumpled on the cold stone floor. Despite the huntsman's orders not to touch anyone or anything, Petra dipped her finger in an open apple pie and then tasted it. The filling was sweet and fresh as if the mixture had been placed inside only minutes before. She ate some more. At least they wouldn't starve while they were here. There would be enough food in the city to keep them going for several hundred years.

An echo of a shout carried its way to her and she frowned, abandoning the pie and running back to wards the centre of the building, her shoes slapping against the floor and raising dust in her wake. Was that danger? The shout came again. Closer this time.

'I've found something. I need help!'

She almost collided with the huntsman as she rounded a corner into the central hallway and with out pausing they both ran up the sweeping staircase, taking the steps two at a time, following the prince's shouts until they found him in a set of luxurious apartments in the middle of the castle.

Petra stood in the bedroom doorway and her mouth dropped open.

'We've got to do something,' the prince said. 'We've got to help.'

Petra cautiously followed the huntsman inside the vast room. At its centre was a large four-poster bed, covered in sheets and blankets of pure, soft white. Sheer linen curtains hung around it, tied back to the posts with ribbons like curtains. In a glass by the bed, a single red rose sat in water, all of its petals scattered around the glass save the last one which drooped low but still clung to the stem. A beautiful young woman lay sleeping on the bed. She was fully dressed in a blue silk gown and jewels sparkled at her neck. Her full lips were parted slightly as if something had just surprised her, and her hair, jet black apart from two thick blonde streaks on either side, spread out across the pillow in glossy waves. She was beautiful, but she was also incredibly pale. Given the state of the floor around the bed, that wasn't a surprise to Petra.

Blood. It was everywhere. A pool of it, thick and crimson, had spread beneath her and now almost circled the large bed. The girl's right hand hung over the side of the bed and as Petra stared at it a single tiny drop of blood fell from her forefinger to the floor.

'It's her finger,' she whispered. 'Look. She must have pricked her finger.'

'Have you got any bandages?' the huntsman asked. 'Any salve?'

'Maybe.' Petra yanked the small bag her granny had packed from her shoulder and tipped the contents out over the end of the bed, taking a careful step to avoid the blood. 'Is she still alive? She must have lost nearly all her blood.'

The prince leaned over the bed and placed one hand on the girl's chest. 'Yes!' he exclaimed, smiling. 'She's breathing.

Just.' He didn't lift his hand though, but ran it up the sleeping beauty's body. 'I've never seen a girl like her,' he whispered. 'She's perfect.'

'I don't think you should be touching her like that,' Petra said as she handed the huntsman a small jar of her granny's natural antiseptic. 'She's asleep. You can't go around touching girls when they're asleep.'

The prince either wasn't listening or chose to ignore her, because as the huntsman cut a strip of sheet from the bed, the prince stroked the girl's face. 'I should kiss her,' he murmured.

'No you really shouldn't.' Petra glared at him. 'That would be all manner of wrong. If someone kissed me without my permission – handsome travelling prince or not – I'd punch them.'

The huntsman laughed. 'She has a point.'

'She's a princess. I'm a prince. I'm *supposed* to kiss her.'

'We need to talk about the dungeons—' the huntsman started.

Two things happened at once. The huntsman wrapped the strip of cloth tightly around the tiny salved cut and stopped the next tiny droplet from escaping the wound; the prince ignored Petra's warning, lowered his mouth to the sleeping princess's and kissed her.

A sudden tremble ran through every stone in the building, and then, as the prince lifted his lips from hers, the girl on the bed gasped and then coughed, and then her eyes opened.

'She's waking up,' Petra whispered. In the glass by the bed, the rose came into full, beautiful bloom. A clattering noise came from somewhere close by, followed by a brief exclamation. Outside, a horse whinnied.

'Not only her,' the huntsman said, getting to his feet. 'They're *all* waking up.'

'We've lifted the curse,' the prince said, his hand still holding the princess's.

As the city came alive around them, all three travellers stared at the beautiful girl on the bed who was slowly easing herself into a sitting position. Colour was rushing back into her face as if with the curse lifted her body was restoring itself to perfect health. She looked at them, her eyes bleary.

'Who are you?' her voice was soft and sweet. 'What happened?' She looked down at her bandaged finger and the blood on the floor below and her eyes widened, her confusion gone. 'There was a spindle! Rumplestiltskin!'

'I'm a prince from a faraway kingdom,' the prince said. 'My father had heard legends of your city's plight and we came to save you.' Petra could clearly see that the young prince was in the process of falling head over heels in love. 'I woke you with a kiss,' he finished.

The woman on the bed smiled at him and either chose to ignore the fact that the bandage was more likely to have saved her than a stolen kiss, or wasn't awake enough to think it through properly.

'How long have I been asleep?' she asked.

Petra thought of the lines that had been scratched into the statue at the centre of the sleeping city.

'We think nearly a hundred years,' she said softly.

The princess said nothing for a long moment and then, just before the soldiers burst into the room, she muttered that one word again.

'Rumplestiltskin.'

5

'Tonight is for celebration'

As it turned out the princess wasn't a princess at all but a queen, and her name was Beauty. As the city woke from its slumber she declared the day a holiday and ordered the kitchens to prepare a great feast to celebrate. She was a whirlwind of light and laughter and the huntsman saw that the prince was dazzled by her. She, in turn, seemed quite taken with him, and she kept her arm linked with his as she walked through the castle with her guests.

'My poor father, the king, has only been gone six months,' she said. 'We were a city in mourning but now we must put that behind us and look to the future.' She looked up at the prince and smiled. 'And I can't thank you enough for saving all of us from this terrible curse.'

'We— I –' the prince said, '– am your humble servant.

I would have slain a dragon to save you.'

'But why would anyone want to curse you?' Petra asked.

'I don't know,' Beauty answered. She frowned. 'I can't remember. I just know that it was Rumplestiltskin.' Her voice was soft and her frown deepened into puzzlement. 'Uncle Rumple.'

'Your uncle?' the prince said. 'But that's terrible. He must want the crown for himself.'

'I called him my uncle,' Beauty said, 'but he wasn't a blood relative. He was my father's closest advisor.' Her frown dissolved into sadness. 'I thought he loved me.'

'Everyone loves you, your majesty.' A middle-aged man dressed in heavy, fur-lined robes swept along the corridor towards them. 'You must never forget that.' When he reached them, he bowed deeply. His dark eyes were sharp under his bushy eyebrows. 'Let your faithful advisors worry about such things. He will not get close to you again, that much I personally guarantee. For now, you should put it out of your head and be glad that such a dashing prince has restored all to order.'

He smiled at the prince who beamed back, happy to be at the centre of such adulation, but the huntsman caught the sharp edge to the older man's smile and the hint of nervous energy escaping from him.

'Thank you, First Minister.' Beauty said. 'You have always been so very good to me.'

'That's because I know and understand you, your majesty.

Let your council worry about such things; you should all be bathing and preparing for the feast,' her advisor continued. 'Tonight is for celebration!'

'You're right.' The queen rose up on tip toes and gave the man a kiss on his bearded cheek. 'You are so often right. I just wish I could remember. There are always so many things I can't remember.' She clapped her hands together, her smile restored. 'But let us retire to our rooms and prepare. Later there shall be music and dancing and everything will be well in the world again.'

The huntsman let the small group walk ahead and hung back with the advisor. 'What does she mean when she says there are things she can't remember?' he asked. 'Is she ill?'

'No, no,' the first minister said smoothly, picking up his pace to return the huntsman to the group. 'She has had occasional small memory blackouts since she was a child. They are nothing unusual. Nothing to concern you.'

The huntsman smiled and followed him, but his skin prickled. He might not be a man of court, but he was pretty sure that whenever someone said there was nothing to concern him, it meant exactly the opposite.

The huntsman did not take much time preparing for the dinner, choosing to keep his own clothes on after washing rather than wear the fancy shirt and trousers left for him in his room. These people were not his people and while he would be polite and respectful, he had no desire or need to impress them. As far as he could tell his job was nearly done. He just needed to get the prince safely home again.

He catnapped for half an hour or so and then wandered the castle and grounds for an hour. After the stillness and silence of their arrival it was strange to see the people suddenly active, like dolls brought back to life. Did they even know how long they had slept, he wondered, as women scrubbed dust from the floors and men polished windows. Most were laughing and talking excitedly, but here and there some cast suspicious looks his way and kept their heads down as they scurried to their next task.

In the central corridors of the castle he passed groups of gentlemen and ministers, each dressed like the first minister but with perhaps less fur and finery on their robes. A few were huddled in deep conversation, only breaking away and pretending mirth and laughter as he went by. Were they plotters, he wondered. The young queen was sweet and kind; were these old men trying to take her kingdom from her? He tried to push the thought from his mind. This was not what he was here for. This kingdom's problems were none of his business.

He climbed high up into one of the turrets, wanting to get a view of what lay to each side of them, but as he reached the summit he was stopped by two soldiers. They were not boys, but men; thick set and gruff. Beyond them, a large black bell hung in a recess.

'You're not allowed up here,' the largest of the two men said. 'Everyone knows that.' His hand was on his sword, and the huntsman raised his hands slightly.

'I'm just a visitor,' he said. 'I wanted to see the view.'

'Then use the windows. This tower is out of bounds. Only the ministers are allowed up here.'

They took a step forward and the huntsman retreated back down the stone stairs. Why would a bell need guarding? Why did he get the feeling that this castle was filled with secrets? There was only one person who could give him the answers: the traitor Rumplestiltskin, wherever he was.

The moon was full that night and the windows were wide open to let the light shine through; the feast was a merry affair. The sumptuous banqueting hall had been decorated with flowers and candles and every table was filled with more food than the guests could possibly eat. The huntsman and Petra sat to either side of Beauty and the prince, who really only had eyes for each other and spent most of the evening holding each other's hands and feeding each other sweetmeats.

Petra, dressed in a beautiful red gown and looking every inch the court lady, was talking to a minister seated on the other side of her while the huntsman, not one for small talk at the best of times, ate and drank while quietly watching the gathered guests. They were mainly older men and women and although they smiled and laughed, he noticed that they did not look often to the main table where their queen sat.

'Some more wine, sir?'

The huntsman looked up to see a pretty serving girl smiling at him. He nodded and she leaned forward to refill his glass, angling her body so that her ample cleavage was clearly on display should he choose to look. Being a hot-blooded man of the forest, he did. 'Tell me,' he said. 'Who are all these guests?'

'Ministers and their wives mainly,' she answered. 'Friends of the old king. Why do you ask, sir?' She continued to lean forward intimately and he could smell her clean warmth and her young skin was clear and bright.

'They just all seem a little old for the queen. Where are all the young men of the court?'

'Oh, they don't come to these dinners, sir. They come to the balls. I don't serve at the balls so I can't tell you about them.'

The flirtation in her voice was replaced with a slightly defensive edge, but the huntsman squeezed her hand and winked and the blush returned to her face. Suddenly he felt the need for something simple and uncomplicated and this girl was clear about her attraction to him.

'Perhaps, after the feast,' he said, 'we could drink some

wine and I could tell you a few things about my homeland.'

'I'd like that.' The girl grinned. 'I'll find my way to your rooms then.' She turned and bustled away and the huntsman smiled after her. Courtly intrigue he could live without.

'Hey.' A finger tapped his shoulder and Petra snuck into the seat beside him. 'The forest hasn't opened up.'

'What?' The huntsman was still wondering how the serving girl would feel beneath him. Petra nudged him again.

'The minister I was talking to. He said that the forest wall is still there. The curse or whatever it is can't have been broken fully.' She paused. 'Is it just me, or does everything seem a bit odd? Bits of this castle just don't make sense.'

'It's not just you,' the huntsman muttered. 'I saw the dungeons—' But before he could say any more the prince got to his feet, tapping the side of his crystal wine glass with a small spoon. His face was flushed and his eyes sparkled.

'Firstly, I would like to thank you all for this wonderful hospitality you have shown me and my travelling companions. We are honoured and humbled at the kindness you have shown us.'

There was a smattering of applause and the huntsman nodded awkwardly at the guests who caught his eye.

'But my biggest thanks must be for the beauty that you have brought into my life.' The prince looked down at the smiling woman beside him and suddenly the huntsman knew where this speech was going. The prince was headstrong and impulsive, he'd already known that, but foolish was about to be added to the list.

'From the moment I saw her asleep on her bed, I knew I would love her forever. I had never seen anyone so perfect,' he said. 'I have asked her if she will marry me,' he smiled at the guests, 'and she has said yes.'

A few gasps ran round the room and then the assembled ministers burst into applause. The huntsman watched as a few of the men exchanged glances as they clapped. Behind their smiles, they weren't entirely happy with the news...

'And so,' the queen got to her feet, 'let there be music and dancing!'

It was when the young couple were on their third dance that the first minister signalled the huntsman and Petra to follow him to an ante-chamber and closed the door behind them. He poured them each a glass of red wine and then sat behind a heavily inlaid desk. The huntsman wondered if the young prince realised who really ran this kingdom. It wasn't the pretty girl he was dancing with, that was for certain.

'I want you to undertake a task for me,' he said. 'Your prince has said I may count on your agreement.'

For the thousandth time since leaving his home, the huntsman once again silently cursed the prince.

'My job,' he said, leaning against the wall and sipping

his wine, 'is to protect the prince and ensure his safe return. Nothing more.'

'Then you will do as I ask. For I imagine his safety depends on it: you must find Rumplestiltskin and bring him to me.'

'Don't you have soldiers who can do that?' Petra asked. 'You do seem to have a lot of soldiers here.'

'The soldiers are looking for him too. But I have my reasons for wanting you to find him rather than them.'

'Why?' the huntsman asked. He thought of the dungeons but didn't mention that he'd seen them. Somehow he thought that might blacken his card and, as Petra had pointed out, there were a lot of soldiers in the city. It wouldn't be difficult for the first minister to dispose of a travelling huntsman. And nor did he want to end up on the wrong side of one of those cell doors.

'Just to be certain,' the first minister smiled, hiding an impatient flash of an expression behind it.

'You don't think he was working alone,' Petra said. 'You want names from him.'

'My reasons are none of your concern. Suffice to say that I want him brought to me and the spindle he carries destroyed.' He took a thick piece of parchment from the desk and handed it to the huntsman. 'Those are the addresses of his home and other places he frequents. Perhaps you'll find clues to his whereabouts there.'

The huntsman took it and tucked it into his belt. 'We'll try, but we don't know your city or its people. The soldiers will have more luck.'

'You're a huntsman,' the first minister purred. 'Hunt.'

'We'll wait until the city is asleep,' he said, 'and go then.' He opened the door for Petra and they left the minister behind.

'He thinks there are other conspirators,' Petra said. 'Why would anyone conspire against Beauty? She seems the kindest and gentlest of creatures.'

Without consultation, neither of them headed back to the banqueting room from which music and laughter drifted towards them, but took the central staircase up to their rooms.

'Who knows?' the huntsman said. As they turned onto a vast landing the curtains billowed in the evening breeze coming through the open veranda doorways. Petra paused and her gaze drifted, as if their current conversation was suddenly forgotten. 'Did you hear that?' she asked.

'What?' the huntsman frowned. His hearing, trained by years of tracking, was excellent but aside from the revellers below and the breeze the air was empty.

'Oh nothing,' Petra said softly, heading towards the balcony doors. 'Just something I've heard before. From the other side of the wall.' She pulled the curtains back and stood in the open doorway. Outside the moon shone full and low in the dark sky. 'I think I'll sit out here for a while. Get some fresh air.'

'You don't have to come with me tonight,' the huntsman said. 'You may be safer in the castle.'

'I want to come,' she answered. 'There's something in this city I need to find too.' She glanced back at him over her delicate shoulder, her eyes dark in the gloom. 'And I'm not at all sure how safe this castle is.'

He couldn't argue with that. His own senses had been humming ever since the queen woke up and the first minister's request made his nerves jangle. He was already a pawn in one royal court's game, and now he was embroiled in another. As Petra wandered out towards the edge of the balcony, he left her and took the stairs two at a time, needing to release some energy.

A figure waited outside his bedroom door. He frowned and then smiled. It was the serving girl. She dropped into a slight curtsey.

'I wondered where you'd gone.' She looked up, her eyes sparkling mischievously. 'I thought p'raps you might like something brought to your room.' She held up a jug of wine. 'I thought I could serve it to you. Personally.'

The huntsman laughed and swung open the door to his room. He bowed. 'Ladies first.'

'Oh,' the girl giggled as she passed him. 'I'm no lady.'

6

'*The dark days...*'

'Perhaps all this was just fate,' Beauty murmured into his chest as the prince held her close and they danced. 'If Rumplestiltskin hadn't done whatever he did, if I hadn't slept, then we'd have never met.' She looked up at him and smiled. It was the sweetest expression he'd ever seen and his heart melted all over again just looking at her exquisite face. Her eyes were the colour of clear water in a summer stream and he wanted to dive into them. To know her completely. 'I would have been long dead before you were born,' she continued. 'You would never have woken me.'

'Then yes, my love.' He kissed her forehead. Her skin was soft and her hair smelled of spring flowers. He was completely enchanted by her. 'It must be fate.'

'You saved me,' she tilted her face up to him, the two

blonde streaks in her perfectly black hair hanging loose in styled curls to either side of her pale cheeks. His lips met hers and they kissed again. She was soft in his arms and the feel of her tongue touching his was electric. He *had* saved her. Already, in his mind, he had pushed aside the image of the huntsman bandaging her finger and stemming her dripping blood at the moment she woke. That was simply coincidence.

'True love's kiss is the only way to break a curse,' she said, her mouth only parted from his by a breath. 'Everyone knows that.'

'And I love you truly,' he whispered back, his voice raw. He did love her. It had gripped him from the moment he'd touched her, a wave of wonder and awe and passion that he'd never felt before. It was almost like magic. He pulled her closer to feel the swell of her bosom against his shirt. His mouth dried slightly as he fought the urge to run his hands over her body.

'Let's get married quickly,' he said. His desire for her was so great he wasn't sure he could wait any longer. Everything else had faded away; his father's wishes for an expansion to his kingdom, the desire to return home laden with treasure and be treated like a hero, even his normal lust for drinking and wenching had gone. Home was a distant memory. All that mattered was this girl and possessing her completely.

'Yes,' she said, as breathless as he was. Her eyes sparkled

in the light from the glittering chandeliers above. 'I will announce it to the city tomorrow and we shall wed the next day. We'll have a family and live happily ever after. I shall give everyone in the city a gold coin as a wedding gift to show my happiness. And there will be days of feasting. I want my people to be as happy as I am. It's all I ever want.'

The prince was sure his heart would explode. Not only was she beautiful, she was kind and gentle and generous too. 'I can't believe that you weren't betrothed already,' he said. 'What is wrong with the noblemen of this kingdom? Or the princes close by?'

'My father was very protective of me,' she said, quietly, a slight shadow darkening her face and her eyes glancing away. She must have loved him very much, the prince thought. 'Well, now I'll protect you,' he said. 'My huntsman will find the traitor and all will be well.'

'And we'll live happily ever after,' Beauty murmured again, her smile returning. They kissed once more and the music played on. Around them, aware that the young couple had eyes for none but each other, the ministers and their wives quietly slipped away. They were no longer young and neither was the night, and despite having spent a century sleeping their bodies were tired and their feet ached and they wanted to let their smiles drop.

A few paused at the door and glanced back with a mixture of nerves and heartache. She was so very beautiful, and so very sweet. And then they shuddered slightly, unable to stop themselves, before heading to their rooms in the castle.

It was a cool spring night, but Petra didn't care. The castle, exquisite as so much of it was, felt claustrophobic, and she couldn't shake the unsettled feeling that had plagued her since Beauty had woken. The prince was blind to it – blind to everything but his sudden love – and even that she found strange. She knew men could be fools where women were concerned, and although the prince was too spoiled and arrogant for her to find him attractive he hadn't struck her as stupid. Her great-grandmother had passed down many tales of handsome princes – stories that were no doubt just flights of fancy – but they had ingrained in her the truth that royals were invariably only true to themselves. This one was suddenly a changed man, if that were the case.

The forest wall was still thick around them. The garish ballroom she'd found while the city slept was now firmly locked. Things were not well in this kingdom. She leaned on the smooth white marble of the balcony and tilted her head back. Above, the moon was full and heavy in the sky, shining its cool light over the darkness of the city below. Music drifted up from the ballroom as the party endlessly continued and she frowned as she tried to listen *beyond* it. It was an irritating distraction from the sound her ears sought.

The counterpart to her soulful duet that had drawn her here even before the prince and the huntsman had arrived in her life. She didn't care about castles and sleeping beauties. She didn't even care about curses. These things were best left to run their course. It was the haunting song which had found her through the thick forest wall that held her here.

There it was. She almost gasped as she heard it; a faint low howl. It sang to her, so full of melancholy and yet so strong. Her heart fluttered. Her skin tingled. She stared out into the night. 'Where are you?' she whispered. '*What* are you?' The howl came again. Animal and human rolled into one. Without a thought to anyone who might hear her, she tilted her head back and answered the call. The creature, wherever it was, let its voice join hers, and she was sure she could hear her own excitement in the sound as their cries mingled in the night. Her feet yearned to run down the stairs and out into the strange city night. The huntsman could find this Rumplestiltskin. She would be on a different search.

The sheets were a tangled mess around their legs and the serving girl, whose name it turned out was Nell, lay on her side next to the huntsman, her hair tumbling over one shoulder. She took a sip of wine and then handed him the glass. 'You must be thirsty.'

He laughed a little and drank, enjoying the sweat cooling

on his body and then leaned forward and kissed her. She had an earthy beauty and a full voluptuous body that might one day swell into fat but for now was young and firm. She smiled and then settled down against his chest, both of them content in the enjoyment they'd taken from each other. They hadn't done much talking, their needs too urgent, but now they were sated they shared that comfortable space that only exists between two strangers who'd just had good enough sex to be at ease in each other's company. Their bubble of intimacy and affection might not last, but it would at least remain as long as their nudity did.

'How long have you worked at the castle?' the huntsman asked, his fingers trailing through her hair and running down the soft skin of her back. She had been no virgin, her forward behaviour had made that clear before anything she'd done, but she was young – no more than seventeen or eighteen – and a bright enthusiasm shone in her eyes.

'Only two weeks.' Her warm breath tickled the hairs on his chest. 'I used to work at the dairy out on the edge of the city. Been there since I was twelve, when my parents were taken by the flu.'

'I'm sorry,' the huntsman said.

'Don't be. It was years ago and the women at the dairy were good to me. I can't complain. Lots of girls there had no families for one reason or another. I wasn't alone in that and it was a good place. The work wasn't too hard once you knew what you were doing, and they weren't too strict.' She giggled a little and then glanced up at him, her eyes full of remembered mischief. 'I used to sleep in a dorm with six other milkmaids. Some nights there were as many men in our room as maids. Sometimes *more*.'

'I thought you'd learned a few tricks from somewhere.' The huntsman pulled her closer, enjoying her uncomplicated warmth. Her past sexual encounters didn't bother him – and wouldn't have even if he had loved her. He had no time for bedroom double standards. It didn't fit with his internal logic and just struck him as stupidity. They were all just animals, after all, and why should a woman deny herself pleasure simply because an insecure man might think less of her? If no women gave in to their lusts then his own life would have been much duller – women were by far the more sensuous sex but most men didn't know how to keep those feelings alive in them. Most men made them feel ashamed of their desires rather than delighting in them and then wondered why everything died and dried up between them. It would not be like that for him, should he ever find the girl in his dreams.

'From the dairy to the castle seems a big leap for an orphan girl,' he said. He was probing her but he couldn't help it. Ever since he'd got here his hackles had been up and soon he would have to go and hunt a traitor – a job he didn't relish if he was working in a situation where he felt blinkered. He was no soldier who could simply obey orders. 'How did you manage that?'

'A few of the dairy girls have come to the castle over the years,' she said. 'The first minister visited and he chose me himself. So I packed up my things and here I am. I sometimes miss the dairy though. Even though life is easier, everything's so much stricter here.'

'You still seem to manage to find your fun, it seems,' he said.

'Well when a handsome stranger comes visiting I have to make the most of it.'

'So life in the kingdom is good then?' he asked, sipping wine thoughtfully.

'Yes, why?'

'There are so many soldiers everywhere. The castle is so heavily guarded. I thought you must have recently been attacked by another kingdom. They're always fighting, after all.' He paused. 'When we arrived and you were all sleeping, I saw the dungeons. Some of the equipment in there is...' It was hard to find an appropriate word for it. He hunted and killed as a way of life, but he made every death as swift and as painless as possible. The things he'd seen here were designed, as far as he could make out, to cause the maximum agony while keeping someone alive. It was the dungeon of a tyrant king, not of a beautiful, happy queen. 'Barbaric,' he said in the end.

'I wouldn't know about that.' She tensed slightly in his arms. 'And there's been no fighting. I think there are so many soldiers because of the dark days. We haven't had one for a month or so. There must be one due.'

'Dark days?' he asked.

'We're not meant to speak of them. No one is. It might upset the queen and no one wants that. She's such a gentle soul.' She sat up, crossing her legs and wrapping the sheet around her for warmth now that their sweat had cooled and heat faded. She took the wine glass from him and sipped. He didn't press her with another question but waited as she drank.

'They say that the queen was one of twins, but her sister was born mad and cruel, and lives locked up in apartments high in the castle. She's been there ever since her father locked her away for the safety of all. Sometimes at the queen's insistence, because she is fair and good and kind and loves her sister despite her wickedness, they change places. The queen locks herself in the apartments and her sister takes control of the castle. A bell rings out over the city and we are all to lock ourselves away until it's over.'

'And what does this other queen do during her time free?' The huntsman was troubled and intrigued in equal measure.

'No one really knows. There are always huge thunder-storms overhead that turn the roads to rivers. They say the other sister has her mother's magic. Sometimes there are parties at the castle.' Her face was animated but not without fear. 'I've heard carriages pass through the streets on those nights. But soon enough the sky clears and the bell sounds again and life carries on as normal.'

'How often do these days happen?' he asked.

'It depends. Although I'm sure they happen more often than they used to.' Nell shrugged. 'Like I said, we don't talk about them. No one would want the queen to know, and she's so kind to everyone. Perhaps there are so many soldiers because the ministers worry that someone might try and hurt her sister?'

It was the same thought the huntsman had. Nell was earthy but she wasn't stupid. A voice cut across the room.

'Well, my dear, now that you've given our visitor a potted history of our city's ridiculous rumours, perhaps you could get back to work?'

The huntsman had reached across the bed for his hunting knife before he realised that the speaker was the first minister. He stood in the corner of the room, his mouth tight with disdain. How long had he been there? It wasn't like the huntsman not to sense a stranger nearby. Maybe they hadn't closed the door to his room properly as they'd tumbled inside.

'I'm sorry, sir.' Nell leapt from the bed, her head down, the sheet wrapped round her as she dropped into a clumsy curtsey.

'She didn't do anything wrong,' the huntsman said, still lounging on the bed, forcing his body to relax so as not to give the statesman any clue how much his sudden interruption without knocking had irritated him. 'I didn't really give her any choice.'

The first minister looked at Nell who, having gathered her clothes, was shuffling to the bathroom door in order to dress with some modicum of modesty. 'Yes. I'm sure,' he said, his tone heavy with irony. 'She looked entirely *coerced* when I came in.'

'I have very strong powers of persuasion.'

'I'm sure you do.' The minister drew himself up tall. 'I hope your hunting skills are as impressive. It's time for you to go and find Rumplestiltskin. Remember, I need him alive.' He paused. 'And remember that your prince is still in the castle.'

The huntsman got up and stretched, enjoying the minister's discomfort at being presented with his nudity, before reaching for his trousers. 'Was that a threat?' he asked. 'When he is so beloved of the queen?'

A sneer crossed the minister's lips. 'Her safety is more important than her happiness. Sweet she might be, but I know her better than she knows herself.'

'But it's still a threat.' The huntsman smiled, his eyes twinkling. He had no time for anything other than plain speaking. The first minister shrugged. 'I prefer to think of it as a reminder of the balance of our relationship.'

'Don't worry,' the huntsman said, pulling his rough shirt

over his head. 'I'll do my best.' He tucked his knife into the sheath on his belt and picked up his bag. He wasn't leaving the diamond shoes behind: there was no one here he trusted not to go through his things, not even the prince. He headed towards the door, deliberately brushing past the older man's slight frame. Not enough to nudge him, but just enough to let him know he wasn't intimidated by him. The huntsman might not have been educated in castle politics but he understood that power play amongst men worked in many different ways, and being the stronger of two was a primal strength.

'One more thing,' the first minister called after him. 'The soldiers.'

'What about them?'

'Don't assume they are friendly.'

The huntsman frowned. 'What do you mean?'

'I can't guarantee they are all loyal to the queen.' The minister steepled his fingers together under his chin. 'Let's just say that there may be some amongst my number who are my enemies. The soldiers are ordered to deliver the traitor to the whole council. There are some there who would use him to try and discredit me. That would not be good for the safety of our queen.' His eyes darkened. 'Or, by extension, of your young prince. I think we can both agree that the boy is too blinded by love to see anything other than wonder in the world at the moment.'

'That will be no problem,' the huntsman said. 'I've yet

to meet someone here I trust. If I find your Rumplestiltskin alive, I'll bring him back to the castle. You have my word.'

He turned his back and strode through the door. He'd be glad to get back in the fresh air, even if he was to be confined by the city. At least most of the population would be asleep and he and Petra would have some peace from the wily ways of the strangers they had awoken.

Plus, despite the addresses and maps the first minister had so thoughtfully provided for them, the huntsman had a pretty good idea where to look.

7

'*The Beast is coming...*'

As they walked through the silent streets Petra could almost convince herself that the city was enchanted again. She wondered how the residents could bear to sleep after their hundred year slumber, but it seemed the whole kingdom had fallen straight back into their daily routine. For them, after all, only a moment had passed.

Night was not that far from day and the sky was shifting to a midnight blue from black above them. Never having been in a city so big before, Petra felt as if she was in a maze. Only the castle dominating the skyline behind them giving her any sense of direction. The huntsman, however, was moving confidently.

'Are we going to this Rumplestiltskin's house?' she whispered. She was back in her own clothes, and she pulled the hood of her red cape over her head as a sudden sharp breeze cut through an alleyway. For the first time she wished her beloved coat was black or grey or some colour that would blend into the buildings around her. In the dawn, with all the colour stripped from the air, she wouldn't escape attention, no matter if a soldier or the traitor they hunted only caught a glimpse of her from the corner of his eye. Not to mentioned drawing attention from the creature whose howls danced with her soul. Fascinated as she was to discover it, her heart raced with the danger. She knew only too well how wolves could rip weaker animals apart. Perhaps the colour of her coat was prophetic.

'Would you be in your house if you were him?' The huntsman answered quietly. 'I think not.'

His tanned face and dark eyes were lost to her as he kept in the shadows, but his feet moved with purpose. Petra trusted him. They made a strange trio – the prince with his adventure and need for a fairy tale ending, the huntsman who was clearly with him under duress, and then her, the forest girl, drawn by a rare sound that should terrify rather than attract her. Three outsiders with no common aim and only their need to get home uniting them.

'But we might find a clue there. To where he's hiding.'

'Soldiers will have searched it already, and no doubt wrecked anything of any use. They're rarely the most subtle of men.' They turned a corner and suddenly Petra recognised where they were: the large market square that sat at the heart of the common people's part of the city. The huntsman led them towards the monument in the middle. 'And I might not know where he's been hiding, but I have a good idea where we'll find him.' He pointed at the lines scratched into its surface. 'Someone was alive all this time. If it was him then the best hunter in the world won't find him. He's had a hundred years to explore this city. He'll know every nook and cranny and secret space in it. But people can't hide forever and this Rumplestiltskin must know that at some point he will be spotted by someone. What would you do if you were him?'

Petra looked at the lines which grew more unsteady with each marker of time. 'I would want to get away. Before the queen got too organised again.' She pulled her cloak tightly round her. 'But where could he go?'

'We got in. I imagine he saw us. If I was him I'd try that spot in the forest wall first.'

'But the forest closed up again behind us,' she said.

'Which is why we have a chance to catch him. And then maybe the forest wall will be kind enough to let us out again.'

'Good luck getting the prince to leave,' she muttered under her breath as they moved on again, at a faster pace this time. 'He's completely under her spell.'

* * *

Petra was out of breath and slightly sweaty by the time they'd followed the road to the city's edge. Here and there they'd ducked out of sight from passing groups of soldiers, but none noticed them, and they made so much noise as they approached that there was plenty of time to find a good corner or shadows to hide in. The huntsman studied the high matted wall of the forest and then smiled. 'Look,' he whispered. Petra followed his gaze. A bronze coin sat in the thick grass. 'A marker. He must have left it here after we came through. Remind him where the place was.' He looked around, scanning the area in the gloom. 'Over there,' he said, nodding towards a cluster of weeds and overhanging branches. 'We'll hide there until he comes.'

She had no real desire to press herself against the forest wall again – the memory of how it had tried to suffocate them on their way in was still fresh in her mind – but she stood behind the huntsman and did as he did. The perfume which enveloped them from behind was almost overwhelming, as if every plant and flower had a place in the wall. There was oak and sandalwood, lilies, lilac and apple blossom mixed with blackberry and the crisp scent of thick green leaves. For a moment, it almost made Petra giddy.

'When will he come?' she whispered.

'Dawn, I think. He'll want more light.'

As it turned out, it was not a long wait. After twenty minutes or so a dark silhouette scurried into view and, peering out between the branches, Petra knew it was the man they sought. He was tall and perhaps fifty years of age, and wore a crimson jacket that had seen better days. He had a heavy looking knapsack on his back from the top of which the tip of a spindle poked out. Petra held her breath as he came closer to them, muttering under his breath and scanning the ground until he reached down and picked up the coin. In his other hand he carried a small axe and, after slipping the coin into his pocket, he began to hack at the thick greenery in front of him.

Petra barely felt the huntsman move. He dropped to a crouch, below Rumplestiltskin's sightline, and moved silently out from their hiding place, working his way in a circle so he came up behind the man. The trees rustled as the axe beat into them, and with the sky slowly lightening a flurry of leaves danced around Rumplestiltskin while he tore at the wall, focused entirely on his task. Behind him the huntsman came closer, slowly and steadily, no sudden movements to alert his prey, until, with only two or three feet separating them, he lunged forward, fluid and agile.

It happened so quickly that Petra barely had time to gasp before the huntsman had spun Rumplestiltskin around and in his moment of shock, taken the axe from him. The man let out a low moan and slumped against the forest wall. Petra stepped out from her hiding place.

'You,' Rumplestiltskin said, his voice clear in the still

dawn as he looked from the huntsman to her and back again. His eyes glistened and shone with despair. 'What did you do? Why did you wake her?'

'We need to take you back to the castle,' the huntsman said. 'This is not our business. You and your peers can resolve it.' Petra was surprised by the kindness of his tone.

'You've made it your business,' Rumplestiltskin wailed. '*You* woke her. It was so close. After all this time, so long a time, a hundred years of waiting. It was so close. And then you woke her.'

Petra kept her distance. She wasn't sure what she'd been expecting but this complete emotional desolation wasn't it. Not after what she'd seen of the other ministers. But then, this man had been awake for the hundred years they'd all slept. What would that do to a person?

'After everything I lost,' he whispered, his eyes filling with tears. 'Everything I foolishly gave up. And then you *woke* her. And now everything is just as it was before.' He looked up at the huntsman. 'You stupid, stupid strangers.'

And then he broke. His shoulders slumped further and as he wept a low moan erupted from him carrying in it a hundred years of loneliness and despair. It was a terrible sight. She'd thought he would beg them to let him go, plead for his life, ask to be saved from whatever punishment awaited him at the castle, but instead he was resigned to it. Looking at the small axe he'd brought with him, that was now tucked into the huntsman's belt, perhaps he had never truly believed he could cut his way free.

The huntsman, clearly moved by the man's plight, stepped forward to put an arm around his shoulders and Petra was so focused on the scene in front of her she didn't hear the footsteps rushing up behind her until it was too late.

Suddenly, she was jerked backwards by her red coat, and as strong arms roughly held her she felt cold, sharp steel against her throat. She let out a short yelp and the huntsman turned, Rumplestiltskin forgotten.

'You'll give him to me now.' The voice was gruff and the breath that hit her cheek was stale. She could feel a metal breastplate against her back and she wriggled slightly to try and break free but his arms were strong. He stank of sweat.

'Why don't you release the girl then, soldier?' the huntsman said. 'We're all on the same side here. We were bringing him back as instructed.'

'He's not going anywhere. I've got my orders. There are more men behind me.' His grip on Petra tightened and she struggled to breathe. 'Kill him now and we might let you both live.'

'Let the girl go. She's done nothing.' The huntsman took a small step forward and held up his hands. 'You do what you have to. But I'm not killing a man in cold blood.'

'Stay back.' The soldier – Petra guessed from the tension in his body that he was young and nervous under his bluster – pressed the knife harder against her neck. Too hard. A sharp pain upon her skin and she yelped again, knowing the knife had nicked her. Warmth trickled down her neck. Blood.

The huntsman froze. And then, from nowhere, it came, bounding over the huntsman and leaping towards Petra with a terrifying, angry growl.

The wolf.

It filled her vision. Thick blue grey fur over a vast, muscular frame. This was no ordinary wolf, like those who scavenged her grandmother's goats. This was ethereal and earthy at once. It was twice the size and its fur shone so brightly that even in the dead light of dawn it seemed to glow. It flew through the air before her. Eyes that burned yellow and sharp teeth behind bared black lips. Claws extending from enormous paws. It was rage. It was fury.

Just before it hit her, Petra thought it was the most beautiful creature she had ever seen. And then the air was gone from her lungs and she was on the ground.

The ball had finished an hour or so before, but the prince and Beauty couldn't bear to part company just yet. The prince was sure he should be tired, but the sheer elation of having found love kept him wide awake. Although they had kissed, many times now, there was an innocence about her that stopped him suggesting they go to her rooms despite the throbbing desire he felt for her. He'd wait for their wedding night and then he'd take her gently and sweetly and their love would not be sullied by haste. She was so pure. After all the serving girls and wenches he'd shared his time with he was now almost ashamed of his past earthy encounters. Perhaps he should have kept himself pure for her. But then princes were supposed to be men of the world, and it was right that he should have experience: she was queen, but he would be master of their bedroom.

As night inched towards day they walked arm in arm, pausing here and there as she pointed out paintings she loved, or pieces of ornate sculpture she had commissioned, and slowly she showed him around her vast home; a castle equal to his father's own in wealth and lavishness. They paused in the kitchens where the night bakers had made fresh bread for the morning, and Beauty's kind words to them made the men blush as she praised them in their work.

Nibbling on hot croissants they wandered back into the heart of the castle and through the ballroom that had so recently been full of music and dancing. He pulled her close and they spun, laughing like children, across the floor until they reached the far door and paused to kiss. She was so natural in his arms and he ran his fingers down her face, brushing them across the tops of her breasts and listening to her sigh and shudder slightly with pleasure. She wanted him too, he could see it in the slight parting of her perfect lips and the haze in her eyes.

'I love you,' she said softly and then smiled.

'I love you too.' And he did. She was perfect.

From the ballroom, she led him into the library, all the walls lined with thousands of books which filled polished mahogany and oak shelves. As shafts of sunlight cut through the windows, Beauty ran from one shelf to another pointing out her favourite stories from childhood; princes who slayed dragons on the Far Mountain, pirate tales from the eastern seas and other tales of love, magic and adventure. As she giggled and promised him that they would read these stories together one day, to their own children, the prince spied a small door in the corner, virtually unnoticeable among the beauty and colour of the books around it. It was wooden, mahogany like the shelves, and as he opened it he was sure he heard the tinkling of distant bells. He looked up to see wires running from the hinges and up into the ceiling. A servants' bell? But why here? This was an in-between place, nowhere you would stop and require refreshments or a fire lit. Why would you? It was simply a narrow corridor. Was the door left over from some conversion years ago? Had the corridor once been part of a different room? He stepped forward, curious.

'Beauty,' he called back to her. 'What's down here?' The corridor was unadorned with any portraits and there was only a plain oak door at the other end. He walked towards it, not waiting for her, and lifted the heavy iron ring handle. He turned it and pushed, but nothing happened. The door was locked.

'I never come down here.' Beauty's voice sounded small, all humour gone from it, and he looked back to see her frowning slightly at the other end of the corridor. 'Why don't we go now? I'm tired. We should go to bed.'

The prince crouched slightly and peered through the keyhole. It was dark but he could just about make out the red of the walls and what looked like heavy black curtains. Gold glinted here and there. 'I think it's another ballroom,' he muttered, before straightening up and turning back to her. 'And you've never seen it? How can that be?'

She had started to tremble a little and her mouth tightened. 'I don't want to be here.'

'But aren't you curious? Surely you should know all the parts of your castle. You are the queen, after all.'

'I said I don't want to be here.' The trembling was becoming more visible and as Beauty backed away from him, she tugged at her hair, pulling strands free from the carefully arranged curls piled on her head.

'What's the matter?' What was suddenly upsetting her? Had someone died in this room? One of her parents perhaps? 'I'm sorry,' he said, rushing towards her. 'I didn't mean to upset you.'

He reached for her, but she stepped away from him. Her

eyes had glazed slightly and he wondered if she even knew he was there. 'Beauty?' he said.

'I don't like it here,' she muttered, and then, without warning, she slapped herself hard across the face.

The prince was so shocked that for a moment he couldn't react at all. Bright red finger marks stained her smooth skin. Only when she lifted her hand to do it again did he reach forward and grab her wrist to stop her.

'What's the matter with you? What is it?'

She hissed at him and struggled to pull away, the trembling turning to shuddering so strong that the prince thought she might be about to have a fit. Perhaps that was it. Her breathing was coming faster and she hugged herself.

Rapid footsteps came across the library, and the first minister rushed towards them, his robes flowing behind him. 'What are you doing here? Why did you open the door?'

'I didn't... I just...' the prince didn't know what to say. The older man pushed him aside and wrapped his arm around Beauty. 'Is she okay?' the prince finished, feeling helpless. She clearly wasn't okay. Not only was she having the strange physical symptoms, but something was happening to her hair. The two blonde streaks at the front were darkening and the rest was somehow getting lighter.

'I'll look after her.' The first minister blocked the prince's view. 'Go back to your apartment. Stay there.' He spoke sharply, his words cutting through the prince's shock. The only man who'd ever spoken to him like that was his father. 'Do not come out until I come and say you can. Do you understand me?'

'What's happening?' the prince asked. He felt like a child again.

'The Beast is coming,' the first minister said quietly. 'Now go.'

The prince did as he was told.

8

'Some kind of terrible magic...'

They left the soldier where he lay, his throat ripped out and his eyes forever staring shocked and surprised at the greying sky, and moved quickly. The man might have been lying that there were others close by but dawn was breaking and soon the city would be alive again. It wouldn't be long before the body was found.

The wolf immediately calmed after its swift attack, standing by the dead man and letting out a long sorrowful howl before padding to Rumplestiltskin's side, its eyes fixed on Petra. The man patted the fierce beast's head and then led the small group away. Petra was staring at the wolf, stunned, and the huntsman grabbed her arm and pulled her along. They had no choice now. He couldn't take the huge wolf on – and nor did he want to. There was something almost noble about its grace and ferocity. Had Rumplestiltskin tamed it? It didn't matter; the wolf had saved Petra, and he trusted animals more than men. Where the wolf went, he would follow.

Rumplestiltskin led them to a large oak tree and crouched to pull up a wooden hatch hidden beneath grass and leaves. 'Get in,' he hissed urgently. The wolf bounded through the dark hole first, and the rest followed. Only once they were sealed up in the dank earth did Rumplestiltskin take a torch from a slot on the rough wall, and light it. Ahead of them was a low tunnel, wooden struts here and there propping up the ceiling. It didn't look overly safe to the huntsman, but he followed anyway, holding Petra's hand in the gloom.

They walked, hunched over so far they might have been better off crawling, for several minutes, until the tunnel opened out into a man-made cave, with a door at the far end and a small hole in the ceiling that let in a shard of natural light from the surface several feet above them.

Rumplestiltskin had clearly tried to make it home and as well as two beds and piles of books there was a table holding a jug of wine, some fresh bread, cheese and a leg of roasted pork.

'If you're hungry, take something,' he muttered, clearing some papers from a chair so Petra, still slightly winded from the weight of the wolf, could sit down. The wolf's arrival and their subsequent flight had calmed him.

'You dug this place out? Yourself?' Petra asked, dabbing

a piece of cloth over the cut on her neck to stem the blood.

'We had nearly a hundred years.' Rumplestiltskin put his knapsack down and sat on the bed. 'Relatively, it didn't take very long.'

'We?' the huntsman asked, and then just as the first ray of sunlight pierced through the narrow skylight, the wolf began to change.

His fur glittered a thousand colours and his yellow eyes widened as he whimpered. Myriad lights lifted from his coat and spun in a whirlwind around him until they were so bright the huntsman had to close his eyes. Even then the brightness made him flinch. The beast let out half a howl and then there was silence.

When the huntsman risked looking again the room was back to normal. The light was gone. So was the wolf. In its place, a man lay on the rough ground. He coughed twice and then sat up.

'That never gets any easier,' he groaned, and sat up, dusting off his white shirt and black jacket. His hair was thick and dirty blond and his eyes were green with yellow flecks.

'You're a man,' Petra said quietly. She stared at him. 'I knew you weren't just a wolf. I knew it. All those times I listened through the wall it was you.' She smiled, and the man smiled back, and the huntsman felt the magic between them. It hummed in the room far greater than the glittering lights had shone.

'You're the girl who howls back.' The two stared at each other with the kind of recognition only people who have never met and yet are destined to be together could share.

'You saved my life,' Petra said.

The man nodded, but his jaw clenched with shame at his deed. 'I'm sorry I killed him,' he said. 'Things are different when I'm the wolf. There are no grey areas. I act on instinct.'

'I'm not sorry you killed him,' Petra said. 'He was going to kill us, after all.' Her elfin face glowed slightly and she trembled.

'Then you're welcome.' Rumplestiltskin had poured the man some water and he drank it and then got to his feet. He bowed to Petra. 'My name is Toby.'

'You've been awake all this time too?' The huntsman asked.

'Yes.' The gregarious grin left Toby's face. 'I was cursed. There was a witch in the city, an older woman, and she fell in love with me. She was a beautiful woman, famed for the diamond slippers that had enchanted many men before me into her bed, and she pursued me relentlessly. But I did not love her and she did not take my rejection well. One night she saw me with a lady of the court and her jealousy overwhelmed her. She cursed me. Every full moon I would spend the nights as a wolf. The first time it happened, my family were terrified. Rumours spread of a wolfman, and I was hunted. I hid in the forest and would only creep back into the city to forage for food and drink. It was on one such trip that the forest formed a wall behind me and the city fell asleep. I can only presume that because I was already cursed, the second curse didn't affect me.'

'Was she sleeping?' Petra asked. 'Will she be awake now?'

'No, I went to her house. She was dead in her bed. Murdered. I wonder if she had picked a man to lure to her bed whose wife's jealousy overwhelmed her fear.' Toby shrugged. 'The city will be better without her. She brought her fate on herself.'

'And I am forever grateful for that, despite your being trapped in this ageless time with me,' Rumplestiltskin squeezed Toby's shoulder. 'I would have gone mad without you.'

'Why didn't you sleep?' Petra asked the old man.

'I caused the curse. The magic doesn't affect he who carries it. Time froze for me, but I did not sleep.' He poured himself some wine and the huntsman noticed his hand was trembling. It had been a long hundred years. But why had he brought it on himself? He seemed a harmless man, unless some natural viciousness had been beaten out of him over the century. It was unlikely. Viciousness grew with bitterness and a hundred years alone would make any man bitter.

'Did you curse the wrong sister?' he asked. 'Surely you didn't mean to attack Beauty.'

'The wrong sister?' the old man smiled, wistfully. 'It was so easy for people to believe that story. The dark days. The second sister. The evil twin. One dark with hints of blonde, one blonde with hints of dark. One so kind and gentle and pure, the other wild and wicked and filled with her mother's magic.'

Somewhere overhead a flash of blue lightning crossed the sky and lit up their cave, and thunder rumbled so hard that the ground around them shook.

Rumplestiltskin looked at the huntsman, his eyes tired. 'There was only one child. They named her Beauty. And beautiful she was. But she was more than that: she was Beauty *and* the Beast.

The young king and his people grieved for their beautiful queen and returned her body to the waters from whence she'd come, but still they stayed bitter, and the king did not blame the spirits of her ancestors for their anger. Being a kind and optimistic man he hoped that one day, when his daughter was grown, they would forgive him for his selfish act of loving the water witch and see that something beautiful could come from the union of earth and magic.

He took great comfort in the infant Beauty, for she was a good-natured baby and rarely cried. She smiled and gurgled in her father's arms and soon, although his heart would never truly mend, the cracks began to heal and he poured his love into his little girl, just as his dead wife would have wanted him to.

All the kingdom loved Beauty. It was impossible not to.

Even the old and cynical ministers' hearts warmed at the sight of her. Goodness shone brightly from her every pore and she loved them all in return. It was her nature to love. For her fourth birthday there was a feast and the whole city rejoiced. She was showered with gifts, given not for political advantage, which was so often the case with royal children, but from the heart. She received so many that she insisted on sharing them with the poorer children of the city, and that just made the people love her more.

The only present she didn't give away was the one that made her eyes sparkle more than any other: a black and white kitten she called Domino, a present from her father's best friend and closest advisor, Rumplestiltskin. Domino was just like her, she said, his hair was black with some blond bits too. She smiled and cuddled him and all was well.

Beauty loved Domino and the cat loved her back. Unlike most felines he did not crave his independence but, like a puppy, would follow the little girl wherever she went and slept curled up on her pillow. Some said – or whispered – it was because Beauty came from witch's blood and all witches had a way with animals, but even those who found the kitten's behaviour odd couldn't bring themselves to think badly of the little princess who was always so full of kindness and love.

Domino died three years later on the first dark day. They did not call them dark days then, and none had any idea how dark they would become, but it was the first time that Beauty changed. There was no trigger for it. Perhaps if her mother had still been alive, she would have known what to do with her child to make it better. But the water witch was dead, and the half-child princess was alone in the world of men.

It was a perfect day and the princess had finished her music and dance lessons and returned to her rooms to play. Thankfully, her servants were dismissed and she was alone.

It was the king and Rumplestiltskin who found her and for a while it would be their secret to bear. They had planned to take Beauty riding, but the clear summer day had suddenly grown cloudy and rain had burst from the sky. The king, perhaps be cause of the loss of his beloved wife, was protective of Beauty's health and decided that they would stay inside and play cards instead. The two men were laughing together when they opened the doors to her apartment.

The laughter stopped immediately.

All the king could see was blood.

At first he thought the blood was Beauty's and he ran towards her in panic, ordering Rumplestiltskin to fetch the doctors. But then, as he got closer, he saw the bloody sewing scissors and Domino's glassy eyes staring up from the mess in his daughter's lap.

'His fur wouldn't change,' Beauty snapped, her voice sharp and irritated. 'His fur wouldn't change. And he scratched me.' She was indignant and her normally beautiful face was screwed up so tightly it was ugly. 'He scratched me.'

'What have you done, Beauty?' the king asked in horror, unable to absorb what was so clearly in front of him. He crouched and took the wrecked, lifeless body of the beloved cat from her.

'Look at her hair,' Rumplestiltskin said, having closed the door and locked it to prevent any passing servants from seeing the awful sight within. 'What's happened to her hair?'

'His hair didn't match mine,' Beauty muttered, although she now sounded slightly confused. With bloody fingers she pulled at her own locks. 'He wouldn't change it. Why wouldn't he change it? Why did he scratch me?'

Her hair, which was normally black with two blonde streaks of her mother's colouring, had reversed, leaving her head a cool blonde with midnight stripes on each side of her cherubic face.

'This isn't right,' Rumplestiltskin said, grabbing a towel and wrapping the dead cat up in it. 'This isn't our Beauty.' For she was more than just the king's daughter, she was loved by them all. 'Is this some kind of terrible magic?'

'Daddy?' Beauty was frowning now, looking up. 'Daddy, what are you doing here?'

Her hair began to change again, returning to its natural state, the two opposing colours bleeding into each other, and through the window the first shard of sunlight cut through the rain, the weather changing with her.

The king swept his daughter up and took her into the

bathroom. 'Get rid of that cat,' he growled. 'Where no one can find it.'

Rumplestiltskin did as he was told. There were plenty of places he could have thrown the stabbed and half-skinned animal, but he found a quiet place in the orchard and buried Domino. He had been a good cat and he had loved the young princess well, and Rumplestiltskin, a kind man with a daughter of his own, felt responsible for the animal's fate. A little sweat was not too much to give him. That and a grave where the foxes couldn't scavenge his corpse in the night.

By the time he got back to the princess's apartments, she was washed and changed and sitting on the bed playing cards with the king. She looked up and smiled, all light and laughter again.

'Have you seen Domino?' she asked. 'I don't know where he is.'

From where he stood in the doorway, Rumplestiltskin could see that the king had hastily rolled up the bloody rug and shoved it under the bed.

'He's probably gone to the kitchens,' the king said. His face was a picture of forced normality, his smile stretched across his face as if it were on a rack. 'Maybe he wanted some milk.'

'That's probably it,' Beauty said, but Rumplestiltskin could see the worry on her pretty face for her missing pet. 'I just wish I knew where he was. I don't remember him leaving.'

'He'll be back,' Rumplestiltskin said cheerily as he sat on the bed. 'I'm sure of it.' Inside, he felt a small part of him die with the lie, the first of what he feared would be many, many lies, and life in the castle had changed that day. Of course the change in her had been magic. But it was a magic that she held. This was nothing to do with the witch and her talk of spindles. Beauty was cursed from within.

Beauty was inconsolable for weeks when Domino, rotting in the orchard, failed to return to her. Everyone searched for him, but the little cat was of course not found, and although she missed him terribly Beauty had the resilience of a child and her nature was too full of joy to hold onto her sadness. Eventually she stopped asking after him and life moved on.

The king and Rumplestiltskin remained watchful and stayed close to the princess as best they could to watch for the signs of change. The instances were at first so rare that, for a few years, they did not cause too much consternation, the two men simply sweeping up the child and locking her in her rooms until the skies outside cleared of rain and they'd know that their good girl had returned to them.

They chose her maids carefully but even so, after a while, there were rumours that another child was in the castle, a blonde girl uncannily like Beauty but who huffed and puffed and stamped her foot.

Being a wise man, and knowing in his heart that now

that a door had unlocked inside Beauty it would stay that way, Rumplestiltskin didn't try to quell the rumours. Instead, he added one to circulation – that there had been two babies born to the king and queen. Twins. But the second girl was a difficult child who needed special care and the king had chosen, for her own sake, to keep her out of the limelight that came with being part of the royal family. When the rumour was whispered back to him he knew he'd been successful. Should anything untoward be seen then Beauty would not be blamed and that was all that mattered.

The king hoped that as Beauty grew her changes would become less frequent, but it was a false hope. The princess reached puberty late, but as soon as she woke, bloody, just after her fifteenth birthday, things grew worse.

The changes became more frequent. And when the other girl was in charge, she now had all her mother's repressed magic at her fingertips. It was no longer possible to lock her away in a room until the moment passed, and instead of simple thunder clouds in the sky, blue lightning would crack across the city and rain would flash-flood the streets. She was wild, this blonde girl who ran, laughing and dancing wantonly through the castle corridors, tipping trays of food from servants' hands as she went.

She whipped the stable boy to within an inch of his life for not polishing her saddle well enough, and the king caught her half-naked with one of his ministers.

The man went to the dungeons for that.

That was a mistake.

The princess followed. Not to save him, but to watch the punishment.

She liked blood.

Rumplestiltskin caught her once in the butcher's yard at the back of the castle, her hands buried in the hot entrails of a freshly killed deer. Her eyes were glazed, and as he pulled her away she licked her fingers. He didn't tell the king that. His precious Beauty, Rumplestiltskin feared, was also a monster.

The changes did not last long, a day or two at the very most, but they were impossible to hide. Rumplestiltskin amended his rumour to say that Beauty insisted her sister had the run of the castle in her stead for a few days here and there, and although some in the kingdom believed that, the king could not keep the secret from his ministers any longer. But there was no other heir, and for all her wildness and streak of cruelty, the Beast, as she became known on those days, still loved her father, and was always affectionate towards him and Rumplestiltskin as if Beauty, locked inside her, had that much control over both of them.

The king had a bell installed high in the castle roof, and proclamations were sent out around the kingdom that when it rang all the people should go to their houses and stay inside until it was rung again. The criers claimed it was to protect them from the terrible blue lightning that spat at the ground during these times, and the dangerous floods, and although it was the nature of the people to do as they were told, rumours were still rumours and there was talk of a monster in the castle and magic at play.

It worked for a while. Several years passed and the kingdom and the castle settled into their new routine. Beauty became a young woman her father could be proud of and everyone continued to love her. She was still kind and thoughtful and full of joy. Young men came to court her. One kissed her and fell so passionately in love that when she told her father she didn't love him the boy hanged himself.

When a second kissed her and also fell completely in love with her – although with less disastrous consequences when she rejected him – Rumplestiltskin and the first minister broached the subject of magic once again to the king. Her mother's magic was not just contained within the Beast. Her kisses put men under a spell, and perhaps, although none could argue that she was not the sweetest of girls, there was a little magic involved in the unconditional love everyone who met her felt.

They decided this was a good thing. It would protect the princess from any who might harm her because of the Beast, and the king took to touring the city with her to ensure that she had all of their subjects' love. There was, he reminded them all, no other heir for the kingdom, and the king refused to even consider marrying again. Things continued in their strange new normality.

But as with all things that we pretend are not so bad as they seem, there comes, for each man or woman, a breaking point.

For Rumplestiltskin it was the poisoning of the king.

He had been growing sicker for a while. At first the changes were not noticeable; just a day or two of feeling off colour, a general tiredness, a reluctance to ride. These times came and went and none of the ministers thought anything of it. He grew thinner. Rumplestiltskin and the first minister noticed that the Beast, when she was in residence, was more affectionate towards her father and this caused them both to be suspicious. They kept her from the kitchens when his food was being prepared and she was followed at all times to ensure she did not go near his wine or water.

They saw nothing suspicious. Perhaps the king was just going through a bout of ill health.

It was a summer's day when Rumplestiltskin found Beauty in the orchard picking apples from a tree. He did not look down at the flattened piece of earth close by where her forgotten childhood companion lay buried. She smiled at him as he asked her why she needed so many as she carried in her basket, and said she was baking apple cakes for her father and had been doing so for weeks. He liked them and that made her happy. Her eyes were clear *and her face shone. She was innocent. She was sweet.*

Rumplestiltskin was suspicious. For if Beauty lurked within to protect her father and Rumplestiltskin when the Beast was in charge, logic dictated that the Beast likewise lurked within Beauty.

He watched her from the shadows beyond the kitchen door as she baked. She sang sweetly to herself as she peeled and cored the ripe fruit and prepared the dough. He chided himself for his dark thoughts. There was nothing amiss here – she was still entirely their Beauty. He lingered though, for he was a thorough man, and as he loved Beauty he also loved his best friend, the king.

Just as the cakes were ready to go into the oven, with Beauty's face covered in an endearing dusting of flour and sugar, a dark cloud passed across sky and the room darkened. Beauty frowned, suddenly confused. She had opened the heavy oven doors and had the tray in her hand, but she paused. She turned, returned to the table and put it down. Her eyes were glazed and lost as she reached into her pocket and pulled out a small vial of liquid, tipping a tiny drop of brightness onto each cake. Once the vial was again out of sight, she picked up the tray again.

The cloud passed and life returned to Beauty and she began to hum once more, closing the door and letting the cakes bake. She smiled, content in her work.

Rumplestiltskin slipped silently away, shivering in

horror, his worst fears confirmed. He did not blame Beauty. She didn't know what she had done. But still, the danger was there. As she grew, who would win the battle there? Beauty or the Beast? He could not watch her forever. One day he would not be able to foil her efforts.

Separate batches of apple cakes were made that the king could eat in front of his daughter to keep her happy without being poisoned, and when the bell rang and the Beast came, he would walk a little hunched over and feign some illness.

But the king was troubled. He had grown into a wise king and he knew that above all else his loyalty should lie with his people. There were talks long into the night of what should be done. The Beast grew wilder and less controllable, and her visits more frequent. The king knew that she went to the dungeons and arranged terrible punishments for the prisoners there, then bribed the guards not to speak of it. None would argue with her. It only took one guard to be punished to show the rest that she was not to be disagreed with. She had magic, after all. Worse, there were those among the nobles, Rumplestiltskin could see it, who almost admired her ruthless nature and brought their sons and daughters in to be her companions, and curry her favour. As Beauty herself was divided, she was also dividing those around her. The good and bad in people became more pronounced and factions grew in the court where there had been harmony before.

The king loved Beauty, but he could not love the Beast. He wept for the water witch and for what their love, which should never have been, had created. When his tears were dry he summoned Rumplestiltskin, his most trusted friend, and asked him to go to the witch in the tower and beg her to help Beauty. Perhaps magic could fight the dark magic in his daughter – perhaps the witch would have a power to ensure that the dark days ended. He told Rumplestiltskin to give her whatever she demanded in return, if she could find a way to free his daughter from the curse of her nature.

It was the end of summer when Rumplestiltskin left, taking his own daughter with him. She was uncomfortable in court life and although she had been friends with Beauty when she had been little, after Domino's death Rumplestiltskin had slowly removed her from the princess's company and sent her to a school on the far side of the city. Now she was grown she was out of place amid the stylish confidence of the nobles, and he feared this would mark her as a victim for the Beast while he was away as she took great pleasure in taunting those whom she perceived to be weak.

It was a long journey to the white tower that rose above the trees in the distance, one not without its own adventures, and as they drew closer both Rumplestiltskin and his daughter were in awe of the height of the edifice. There were only two windows they could see, one halfway up and another far away at the very top that would no doubt be lost from sight in the misty days of winter.

There was no visible door and after exploring the perimeter and seeing no way in Rumplestiltskin called up to the window in the hope that the witch would hear him and come down. He shouted himself hoarse, but there was no response. He began to think that perhaps this was a wild goose chase and the witch was long gone or dead within the impenetrable walls. He sat on a rock, ready to give up, and then his daughter shouted for him, begging the witch to show them mercy and hear their plight.

A door, previously invisible, swung open in the smooth curved wall. The witch smiled and invited them in. Rumplestiltskin was not sure what he had been expecting, but she was unchanged – an ordinary middle-aged woman. As they followed her up the winding stairs inside, however, he caught glimpses of artefacts and objects that were hundreds of years old. She noticed his glance and smiled.

'A witch's years are different to a man's. I've stopped counting them.'

She fed them a hearty broth, settled Rumplestiltskin's daughter down on a soft couch to sleep, and then listened to his tale of Beauty and the Beast. The witch was thoughtful after that. She hadn't been out in the world since the king had summoned her, before Beauty's birth, and after hearing his tale she was glad of it.

'A water witch's daughter,' she mused, 'should only be

born from a water bed. This trouble is one anyone could have seen coming.'

She sat by the fire for a while and watched Rumplestiltskin's daughter sleep, as if that sight brought her some clarity or peace, and then made her decision.

'Can you help?' Rumplestiltskin asked. 'I fear for our land if the Beast can't be controlled.'

'Come with me,' she told him. They climbed two more flights of stairs until they came to a room with several locks. 'I have something for you.'

It was full of spinning wheels and spindles of different shapes and sizes and Rumplestiltskin's eyes widened. 'Spindles. Beauty's curse.' The witch smiled. 'They are each bewitched or blessed or cursed, depending on how you use them.' She walked between them, her fingers lovingly caressing the wood of each until her hand settled on one. 'I cannot change her nature,' she said, eventually. 'She is who she is, and no magic is strong enough to change that. But I can save your kingdom from her inevitable tyranny.'

Rumplestiltskin stared at her. 'How?' he asked, his mouth drying. He knew the answer before she spoke and his heart was heavy with the decision he would have to make.

'I can give you something which will kill her, should you feel that is your only recourse.' She turned to Rumplestiltskin and in the candlelight he was sure he could see hundreds of years of life in her eyes and a dead heart beating inside her.

No good came from magic, his conscience screamed, and he trembled slightly. She looked so very ordinary but in her soul she was a crone. No good could come from a crone. 'This,' she said, and lifted one of her precious spindles.

'How does it work?' he asked, after swallowing hard. Ever since Domino he had known that one day a decision would have to be made about Beauty. And somewhere in his soul, and in his love for the king, he'd known it would be his decision to make. 'And will it be painless?' He paused. 'We all love her, you see.' He wondered if he was justifying his actions to himself or to her. 'Hopefully, I will never have to use it.'

'I will need it returning,' she said. 'Especially if you decide some less extreme action is called for.' She carefully lifted it and handed it to him. 'One prick of her finger and she will die,' she said, her voice devoid of emotion. 'And it will be painless. Like going to sleep.' She smiled at that.

'It's poison then,' Rumplestiltskin said.

'She'll bleed to death,' the witch replied. 'But I assure you she won't feel a thing.'

His hands trembled as he took it. 'I must be sure not to prick myself on the way back then.'

'I've given you this magic,' she said, leading him out of the room and locking it with the keys that hung from a chain around her neck. 'It can't hurt you. A curse cannot touch the one who wields it.'

'And what do you want in return?' he asked.

'You will leave your daughter with me until you bring my spindle back,' she said, softly.

Rumplestiltskin felt as if all the air had been sucked from his lungs. His daughter? His only child?

The witch squeezed his hand. He was surprised at the warmth of her fingers. He'd expected them to feel like the touch of a dead thing. 'She will want for nothing and I shall teach her many things. She will be happy here and I am lonely. I have been lonely for a long, long time.' She smiled again. Her lips were thin. 'And when you return you may reclaim her if you so wish. This I promise you.' She shrugged. 'Perhaps she will also be safer here. Dangerous times lie ahead.'

Rump(l)estiltskin felt the weight of all his responsibility to the kingdom settle on his shoulders and his heart grew heavy. He had no choice.

'I will come back for her,' he said.

'I'm sure you will,' the witch replied.

He did not wait for his daughter to wake because he knew he would not have the strength to say goodbye, but left her a letter telling her he loved her very much and that he would return soon to take her home. He kissed her forehead and left his darling daughter, Rapunzel, there where she slept.

By the time he got back to the kingdom two months had passed and much had already changed. The king was dead; killed in a riding accident while out with the princess a mere day after Rumplestiltskin had left. While Beauty mourned for her father, the Beast revelled in her new power. She held masked balls for the wild young things of the city and took her vicarious pleasure not only from their bodies, but also from torturing those unfortunate enough to be in the dungeons. If there were no prisoners there, they were brought in, innocents chosen at random to feed her blood lust, their houses wrecked and looted by the soldiers knowing they would not return.

She redecorated the third ballroom to suit her tastes; decadent red and black and gold, and music played long and loud as the young people danced and enjoyed each other, and girls from the dairy came and never left again alive.

The ministers kept these secrets and managed the kingdom around her as best they could until the bell rang once again and they could let out a collective sigh of relief. None challenged her because her mother's magic was at her fingertips, and they had seen the unrecognisable bodies that left the dungeons. They kept their own counsel and shuffled around the castle trying to look invisible as they did exactly as they were told. With the king gone and Rumplestiltskin away, only the first minister had the true affection of their queen and they left the management of the Beast to him.

It could not go on, Rumplestiltskin thought, as he held Beauty's hand beside her father's grave and cried with her for his oldest friend. It just could not go on.

Whispers of murders and torture, wild parties and

patricide; that was only two months into the new reign and it would only get worse. Beauty was sweet and kind, but the Beast was stronger, he was sure of that. That Beauty had unknowingly killed the king, he had no doubt. He'd spoken to the terrified stable boy who whispered that the girth on the king's saddle had been nearly cut through and that it had been the princess herself who had prepared his horse for him. Who would be next? Her father's friends?

He sat up late into the night, turning the spindle in his hands. One prick, the witch had said, and that would be that. He wished it could be done while she was the Beast. Somehow that would feel easier. But the Beast rarely slept and her magic would protect her from danger. It had to be Beauty he murdered.

He went to her rooms the next afternoon. It was a beautiful day. The city was full of life. A rose, Beauty's favourite flower, sat in a glass on the window sill. She sat on the edge of her bed and laughed with delight as she reached for the spinning wheel, happy that he'd thought to bring her a gift from his travels, especially a thing she had never seen before in her life, and in that moment where she was joyous he saw her delicate finger touch the spindle.

It was done.

Her eyes widened for the merest moment and then the spinning wheel slid from her hands to the floor and she fell backwards onto her bed. Rumplestiltskin stood and *cried, silently begging her forgiveness, for what seemed like forever, before he laid her out on the bed. He was so absorbed in his grief and guilt he failed to notice the sudden unnatural silence around him.*

He did, however, notice that the princess, one arm flopped over the side of the bed, a tiny drop of blood striking the floor from her pricked finger, was still breathing.

It didn't make sense. Not at first. Not until he'd been outside and to the forest's edge and seen the wall that had grown there. And even then it had taken weeks, maybe even months, for the terrible truth to sink in.

'The witch lied,' Petra said, softly.

'Oh no.' Rumplestiltskin shook his head. 'Witches never lie. But they do speak in riddles. The queen *would* die. She would bleed to death and it would be painless. But she would bleed to death one drop at a time.' He shuddered and sipped his wine. 'Before Beauty's birth, the witch told the king that a spindle would send his daughter to sleep for a hundred years. Her prophecy was not destroyed by my deeds. I brought the spindle. I sent her to sleep as I killed her. She would sleep the hundred years it took her blood to drain from her body and then she'd be gone. A hundred years of waiting. And we were so nearly there, when you woke her.'

'Your daughter?' the huntsman said.

'Long dead now. After a life abandoned and locked away in a witch's tower.'

'Locked in a tower,' Petra repeated, her gaze misty as if she was lost in a different story.

'So why is the first minister so keen that we find you and take you to him? You were doing something that surely they all wanted?'

'If I had succeeded, of course. But I failed. The queen is awake, and there's only one other person who knew of my plan and my visit to the witch.'

'Him?' Petra said.

'Exactly. If I'm captured and the Beast tortures me, he knows I'll have no choice but to give up his name. It's better for everyone if she thinks I acted alone.'

'Shhh.' Toby tilted his head and frowned.

'What?'

'The bell,' Toby said. 'The bell is ringing. A dark day has come.'

Rumplestiltskin looked up at the huntsman. 'The Beast is awake.'

'But what about the prince?' Petra asked. 'He's with her!'

'Hopefully the first minister will look after him,' the old man muttered. 'But I fear he's about to have a very rude awakening about his sweet queen.'

9

'Perhaps he was in a dream...'

The bell rang out from somewhere at the top of the castle, a steady heavy knell, and as the prince stared up at the ceiling of his apartments he shivered slightly while his heart raced. Whatever affliction had struck poor Beauty the first minister had not been surprised by it, but the prince had also seen that he was afraid and that in turn frightened the prince. Much to his own chagrin, he wished the huntsman were here. Surrounded as he was by the kind of luxury he was used to, he still suddenly felt very alone and far from home. He loved Beauty, he knew that to his very core, but he was unimportant here. The way the minister had spoken to him made that abundantly clear.

Blue lightning flashed in jagged lines beyond the window and a moment later an almighty rumble of thunder shook the sky. He was sure the castle walls trembled. He was about to go to the window to look when the door to his rooms opened and the first minister entered carrying a silver tray.

'I know it is early, but you have had a long night and I thought you might like something to eat,' he said smoothly, placing it on the table against the wall. 'And a hot drink to help you sleep.' His smile was tight. 'I'm very sorry to have rushed you away like that, but our beloved queen has occasional fits.' He nodded towards the window. 'They come with the bad weather.' The minister had regained his usual poise, but the prince remembered all too well the urgency with which he'd spoken earlier, insisting that the prince leave. What was he hiding? 'It's unlikely she will be well again today, so eat now and then sleep as long as you wish. Take time to recover from your long journey.'

'I should be with her while she's sick. I am her husband to be, after all. It's my job to look after her.'

'And when you are married of course you shall. But the queen requires privacy at these times – the fits are quite traumatic for her – and you can understand why she might want to keep them private from you at this early stage. She is young and easily embarrassed. Anyway,' he clasped his hands in front of him and they were lost in the sleeves and folds of his robes, 'once this one has passed, which I'm sure it shall quickly, I shall teach you how best to deal with them.

But for now she is well cared for, so eat, drink and sleep. Then you have a wedding to plan.'

His eyes lingered a moment too long on the tray and there was a flash of intensity, almost hidden under the first minister's hooded brows, as he turned his gaze back to the prince.

'Of course,' the prince said, his mouth drying. 'You are right. I was simply worried.' He lifted the goblet and pretended to take a sip. 'I shall see her tomorrow. Perhaps, if she is unwell, we should delay the wedding for a day. We can plan it together so it can be perfect.'

The first minister smiled. 'Perhaps that is wise.'

The prince felt the red wine touch his lips but refused to let it pass. Why would the first minister bring him his food and not send a servant? He was a proud man – the prince had known enough counsellors and politicians to know they did nothing to diminish their status in the eyes of others. The minister must have wanted to ensure the prince received it and was going to consume it, and that meant he had probably added an extra ingredient between the kitchen and his rooms. The prince was spoiled and could be selfish but he wasn't stupid. All castles housed ruthless men with their own personal agendas – what if the first minister had decided that Beauty marrying a royal was not in his best interest? She was sweet and gentle – her husband might not be. Who would wield the power then?

He looked down at the silver plate containing half a

roast chicken covered in gravy and surrounded by potatoes and vegetables. 'That looks delicious. Thank you once again. I think I'll read while I eat it and then sleep if you think that's for the best. But please,' he knew he had to keep some of his urgency. 'Tell Beauty I love her and am thinking of her.'

'I will.' The first minister's eyes twinkled and he bowed before he backed away. 'Remember to stay in these rooms. We like to keep the castle peaceful for the queen while she's unwell.'

'Thank you,' the prince said, and sat at the table, picking up his knife and fork and cutting a piece of the succulent chicken. The first minister paused in the doorway and watched as the prince put the food into his mouth and then quietly closed the door behind him.

As soon as he was gone, the prince spat the meat out and ran to the water jug to rinse his mouth out.

He picked up the plate and wine glass and went to the window. Outside it was dark as night and the storm was raging. As soon as he lifted the catch the glass flew back, propelled by the wind that sent the curtains billowing up around him as if they were suddenly enchanted. He flinched against the torrential icy rain that blasted into his face, and tipped away the food and wine. It fell into the gloomy grey street below as more streaks of blue cracked the sky and stabbed at the city. He pulled the window shut and put the empty plate and goblet back, before closing the curtains and turning out all but one lamp.

There were several old books on a shelf in the corner and he took one and opened it somewhere near the beginning and then lay on the bed, placing the book at an angle across his chest as if he had dropped it there. He closed his eyes. Now all he had to do was wait.

His heart thumped in his chest as the minutes ticked by and the fire in the grate slowly burned down. After a while he thought he might have drifted to the edge of sleep, but was woken by the sound of carriages arriving below. He opened his eyes and where daylight should have been creeping through the gaps in the curtains, instead there was a strange darkness, as if the raging storm had created an artificial night. There was something unnatural about it, and he shivered. Shrieks of laughter carried on the wind as carriage doors closed and people ran inside and away from the rain. The prince was suddenly alert again. Who were these people and why were they arriving? There had been a formal ball the night before and if the queen was ill, and the first minister insistent on peace and quiet, surely none would disobey him? So what was really going on? Did he take advantage of the queen's fits to stage entertainments of his own? Maybe that was it.

He was just about losing patience with lying still when he heard the quiet click of the door opening. He forced his body to relax and dropped his mouth open slightly, taking long, deep breaths. Feet padded softly across the carpet. The prince's eyelids twitched, but he remained motionless. After a moment the feet moved away, and the door clicked shut.

The room once again in silence, the prince kept his eyes shut for several seconds longer, afraid that perhaps it was a trick and the minister was still watching him, but eventually he opened them and let out a sigh of relief that he was once again alone.

Back at the window he looked out at the storm. In the courtyard below sat several carriages made of gold and silver and sparkling with jewels. Noblemen's carriages, he was certain of it. Perhaps the first minister was trying to claim the throne for himself and had called some kind of meeting while Beauty was ill? The question was, what could he do about it? What did he really know about this kingdom?

He turned away and glanced at himself in the mirror. He was tall, and blond and handsome; everything a prince should be. Princes should also be brave and honourable. Princes, he reminded himself, did not sit back politely if they thought the security of the one they loved was threatened. And if there was one thing which was beyond doubt, it was that he loved Beauty with every inch of his body. Being apart from her was a physical ache that he almost couldn't bear. He pulled back his broad shoulders. If nothing else, he was going to explore and see what was going on, and he would talk to her about it when she was better. It wasn't as if the first minister could do any thing to him. He was betrothed to their queen. Soon he would be their king and he would not be manipulated by old men, even if his sweet natured beloved was.

He waited another thirty minutes before creeping out into the silent hallway. He stayed close to the walls and followed the wide corridor until he reached the central staircase. He paused and strained his ears to hear. At first there was nothing, but then he was sure he caught the faintest tinkling of music. Two kitchen hands crossed the central atrium below, their heads huddled together and whispering, and then they disappeared from sight. In their wake, the air carried the hint of roasted meat. They'd delivered food somewhere, but where?

When he was certain there was no one else about, he went quickly down the stairs and headed towards the main ballroom where he and Beauty had danced before. He opened the door a fraction but the space beyond was quiet and empty. He stepped inside. The music was definitely louder here. He jogged across the vast space, his footsteps echoing eerily around him.

The second ballroom was empty too, and he frowned for a moment, before the thought struck him. There was the third ballroom. The locked up room beyond the library that Beauty had known nothing about. Was that where the first minister was entertaining his guests?

He'd passed through the library and reached the door to the small corridor. He opened it a fraction and slid his hand up to keep the bellwire steady before squeezing the rest of his body in. He was in the right place. The music, slightly discordant and darker than any of the jolly tunes that he and Beauty had danced to, was much louder, and above the notes he heard the occasional laugh.

With sweaty palms and a racing heart, he crept forward and lowered his eye to the keyhole but couldn't get a clear view of what was happening inside. The chandeliers were giving off a muted light rather than glittering brightness, and he saw flashes of the red walls and movement of clothes and bodies. From the other side of the thick wood, a woman laughed, a tinkling sound like breaking ice.

His curiosity overwhelmed his fear, and he carefully twisted the handle and quietly pulled the heavy door open an inch to see inside. As his eyes widened, so did the door. All sensible thought tumbled from his mind, and he stared, for a moment completely astonished, at the tableaux that faced him.

The room was smaller than the other ballrooms and with the heavy red and gold decoration and the thick black drapes that covered the windows it seemed to shrink further. A fire blazed in the vast ornamental grate and large candles flickered in sconces decorated with gargoyles that cast strange shadows across the floor. Along one side was a table laden with food; roasted chickens and hares, piles of fruit, and all manner of exotic dishes, but instead of using plates and knives the food had been torn apart by hand and gnawed bones littered the floor around it. Silver jugs of wine were scattered everywhere and the thick rug that covered most of the central area was splashed with red where glasses had been carelessly knocked over. Even without the people, it was a decadent sight. With them, the scene was one of flagrantly wild abandon. Men and women in beautiful expensive gowns laughed and talked in groups, some dancing together, some eating or drinking, but all with a lack of formality unlike any royal ball he'd ever attended. All the guests wore elegant masks across their eyes; some black, some ornate bird feathers, some with beaks and all fitting closely to their young features. None were over thirty, he was sure of that, and whereas they were all handsome and beautiful people, the dark shadows they cut in the candlelight across the floor and on the red walls were strange and gothic, the women flirtatiously and confidently moving among the men; no standing on ceremony or waiting to be approached.

There was more though, and from his place in the doorway the prince felt both aroused and revolted as his eyes moved to the others who were lost in their actions, oblivious to the party around them.

On the low stage angled from a corner, three men,

dressed in black screeched out the strange fiddle music. Two women danced in front of them; but this was no courtly waltz. They swayed slightly, their slim hips gyrating against each other's as they kissed, their eyes half closed and lost in the pleasures of their soft mouths. The taller of the two, a brunette whose hair had fallen free and hung down her back, ran one hand down her partner's body stroking the bodice of her dress, freeing her breast and teasing the nipple between her fingers before lowering her head and flicking her tongue across it. The other girl tipped her head back and gasped.

A little further away, a full figured woman was bent over a chaise longue by the wall. The skirt of her ballgown had been pushed up over her hips and the pale skin of her thighs was visible above the tops of her stockings. She moaned as a man behind her gripped her buttocks and thrust into her, panting loudly with each of his movements and lifting herself up to meet him. After a moment another man, a gold mask across his face, joined them and slid his hard cock into her mouth as he leant backwards and drained his wine. The woman sucked greedily, matching her movements with those of the man behind her.

On the thick fur rug two women straddled a naked man and faced each other, one spreading her thighs across his face, the other his pelvis, and as they ground themselves into him for their pleasure, they leaned forward and kissed between their moans.

Other pairings and groups were dotted here and there, all in some stage of undress as they pleasured each other with wanton abandon. As well as their lust, they were feeling love for each other, these people hidden behind their masks. It was strange and unnatural, but despite his revulsion the prince was throbbing.

One woman was alone in midst of the party, and she moved among the people smiling, pausing to laugh with those still dressed, and trailing one hand gently across the skin of the naked as she passed and when she did so the whole group would shudder with pleasure. She wore a dress so sheer the firm curves of her body were clearly visible beneath it, but none of the revellers made her part of their depravity.

When her tour was complete she stood in the centre of the room and turned slowly, her arms outstretched, sparks of gold flying from the tips of her fingers. The air instantly grew heavier and a wave of something warm and sweet hit the prince where he stood. His head spun as if he'd drunk too much wine too quickly. Suddenly he wanted to be in the room, to be part of this madness that was taking place before him. Unable to stop himself, he pushed the door further open, and the woman at the centre of it all looked up. She smiled.

The prince's heart stopped. How hadn't he recognised her before? It was Beauty. *His* Beauty. Except for her hair – her hair was the wrong colour. What was this? How could his sweet fiancée be part of this? Was it really her? Was it a different girl? The last sober shred of his mind knew he should turn and run, but the strange intoxication that tingled in his blood refused to let him move. He remembered her in the corridor behind him. Her confusion. Her trembling. *Her hair had been changing colour.*

She walked towards him, lithe and supple, her movements like a cat, and her eyes sparkled. His eyes drank in the outline of her breasts, the dark circles of her nipples visible through the sheer cream fabric that floated around her as she moved.

'My darling,' she purred as she reached him. 'I knew you'd find me.' She took his hand and his arm shuddered with sharp sparks of something between pain and pleasure. As he crossed the threshold she closed the door behind him and any resistance he might have had was gone. The air was heavy and filled with a musky scent of sex and magic and he longed to tear himself free of his clothes and tumble to the floor with Beauty, not caring who might see their act of love. He pulled her towards him and kissed her. The surge of passion he felt was greater than any that had come before. What was this? Was she enchanting him? She pressed her body confidently against his, teasing him, and then drew back, wriggling free of his grasp.

'Not until our wedding night.' Her voice was slightly deeper than normal, and although he was sure that this was his Beauty, she was, at the same time, a completely different woman. 'Not for me.' She ran her fingers down his shirt, teasing some of the buttons free as she went. 'I have different lusts to fulfil tonight.'

'What is this?' he whispered, as she led him over to the two dancing women who were now writhing with each other on the floor. 'What are you doing?' Warm hands reached up and tugged him down. He didn't resist. The women made space for him between them and, as Beauty smiled at him, they slid their fingers and tongues under his clothes and his head whirled and he gasped.

'Sometimes,' Beauty said softly, sipping from her silver goblet, 'everyone needs to let the beast inside them out for a while.' She laughed, a sound like a waterfall meeting the sea and more glitter escaped from her fingertips. 'I like to see it. We all have our dark lusts. We should enjoy them.' Somewhere inside him a voice screamed witchcraft and then he was lost in sensation as his hands found firm breasts, and a soft mouth touched his as another explored a far more intimate part of him. And for a while, even his love for Beauty was forgotten.

Time meant nothing as the groups of bodies moved and merged and created new formations, but by the time the first minister brought the serving girl into the room, the prince was covered in sweat and his body ached from both desire and the desire to be free of it. The world was a bleary haze and he felt as if perhaps he was in a dream.

The minister walked, his back stiff, without looking at any of the decadence that surrounded him, until he reached Beauty, who was sitting on a throne from which she could survey all around her. She clapped her hands together in delight as she saw the blindfolded girl he'd led inside.

'A special night!' she cried. 'I shall drink!' From his place on the floor, the prince watched as she leapt to her feet and embraced the man before her. He flinched. 'Her name is Nell,' he said. 'She was talking to the huntsman.'

'Why do you tell me the names?' Beauty frowned, cross. 'I don't care for the names. My guests have had their pleasure and now I shall have mine!'

The first minister nodded. His face was tight, as if he dare not show any emotion he might have. 'I shall wait outside,' he said. 'Your guests' carriages are prepared. I suggest you dismiss them before...'

'Yes, yes,' she snapped, and the first minister took his leave. She clapped her hands together again, louder this time, gathering the attention of the revellers.

'Ladies and gentlemen,' she said, addressing them as if this were any normal ball. 'It has been wonderful to see you all again. A *pleasure*.' The guests laughed at that as they reclothed themselves where necessary, and smiled while seeking out their original partners and preparing to leave. 'We shall have another such evening soon. But for now it's time for you to return home and continue your delights at your leisure.'

The room cleared relatively quickly, as if they were used to the parties ending abruptly, and while many came to say their goodbyes to Beauty and thank her for her hospitality, none paid any attention to the blindfolded girl who was swaying slightly in the middle of the room. Beauty held the prince back with her and when the musicians scurried out, the doors clicked shut and the three of them were alone.

'And now for my pleasure,' Beauty said, smiling at him, her eyes dancing with excitement. Her face was flushed and the prince thought, in that moment, he'd never seen her so aptly named.

She circled the girl, an earthy-looking buxom wench, one hand trailing around her waist and the servant gasped but didn't speak. Was she drugged? What did Beauty want with her? The expression on the first minister's face when he'd brought her in flashed before the prince's mind's eye. He'd looked like a tortured man.

'Pretty Nell,' Beauty said softly. 'They're always so pretty.' She reached down to the silver jug on the table and refilled her goblet and then poured a second for the prince. The red wine looked thick and dark and he stared into it as she drank hers.

'Drink,' she said. Her eyes had hardened and the prince suddenly felt unsettled. He lifted the cup and sipped. The taste was metallic and the substance too thick to swallow easily without gagging, as if his body recognised it before his brain had time to.

'Is this... blood?' he asked, as the awful truth dawned on him.

She smiled at him and he could see where the crimson liquid clung to her teeth. 'This is cold, but soon we'll have warm. Fresh and warm and so full of life.' She clung to him and pulled him close and kissed him, seeking him out with her tongue. The prince's stomach churned. *Blood.* His princess, his Beauty, was drinking blood. *He'd* drunk blood.

Beauty broke away, breathless, and laughed, tipping her head back and then pouring the glass of blood over her, coating herself in it, the sheer material of her dress clinging to her every curve with the weight of the liquid. She dropped the empty goblet and the sound of the metal hitting the ground echoed loudly in the empty room and the serving girl – Nell, the prince reminded himself; she had a name – flinched.

Beauty stroked her face and hushed her, kissing her cheek and leaving bloody marks on her pale skin. She looked at the prince. 'Are you ready?' she whispered, and pulled something from a hidey hole in the side of her throne. The prince nodded, despite his need to run far from this place and vomit. He shivered as she nodded at him to drink more from his cup. Cursing his own weakness, he did. He thought it couldn't get much worse than this. He thought she would want him to have blood drenched sex with the poor girl before him.

It was only when he saw the knife in Beauty's hand and

she folded his own over it and they both held the cold blade to the girl's warm neck, that he realised it was all going to get much, much worse before it got better.

Too late he remembered what the first minister had said before sending him to his room.

The Beast is coming.

The prince's mind had cracked a little by the time it was done and the first minister was leaning over him, his eyes wide with anger and hissing, 'I told you to stay in your room! I tried to ensure you would, you stupid, stupid boy.' The prince cried after that, rocking backwards and forwards as the old man put his arm awkwardly round him and tried to pull him to his feet. His feet slipped under him on the blood and he fell back down.

He couldn't get rid of the taste. He didn't think he'd ever be able to get rid of the taste, or of the images that were burned into his mind. The things the Beast had done to the poor, dead girl.

'Why?' he whispered. 'Why would she do that?' Beauty and the knife. Watching as she... as *they*... and then her terrible dancing in the warm blood, smearing it over herself and him, filling wine glasses with it. Forcing him to drink. Being too weak and afraid to stop her doing any of the terrible things she did.

He groaned and, trying to preserve his sanity, he curled up in a small ball in the corner of his mind. He needed to forget. He *had* to forget.

'Get up,' the first minister hissed again. 'Get back to your room. The bell will ring soon and then the castle will be busy again. You can't be seen like this.'

'The bell?' the prince croaked.

'The Beast will leave now.' The minister forced him to his feet. 'The blood precipitates the change. Our queen will return to herself and she can't see you like this.' He glanced at the blood-soaked woman who was starting to tremble. 'She can't see herself like this. Now go. Burn your clothes. Wash and sleep. Forget this ever happened.'

The prince didn't know whether to laugh or cry at the ridiculousness of the suggestion that this could ever be forgotten. That he could ever be normal again. As if he'd heard the prince's thoughts spoken aloud, the first minister gripped his wrist tightly, his thin fingers digging into his skin. 'You will forget it. Or change it in your mind. It's all you can do.' He glared at the prince. 'Now go.'

This time the broken prince did not hesitate.

10

'A deal like that is worse than a witch's curse...'

It was early evening when the skies cleared and the bell rang out again over the city. The group hidden in the hideaway beneath the tree had slept for a while and then eaten. Petra and Toby escaped to the surface to walk in the fresh air, leaving the huntsman and Rumplestiltskin to talk.

After the fierceness of the storm damp lingered on every surface and the trees glistened green as water dripped from their branches, but although there was a light breeze it was not cold.

'Do you think Rumplestiltskin's story of his daughter and the witch is true?' Petra asked as they walked. 'Or in his fragile state of mind did he just make it up?'

'It's the story he's always told,' Toby slid his arm around her waist as if it was the most natural thing in the world, and Petra believed that it might be. 'I think it's true. Why do you ask?'

'Oh, no reason. No reason that matters right now, anyway. Will you change again tonight?' Petra asked, as Toby glanced up at the sinking sun.

'Yes,' he said. 'There's two more nights of the full moon.' He smiled at her. 'But I've got an hour or so before it'll come on me.'

The city sparkled ahead of them, clean and bright, and Petra stared at it, still fascinated by a sight so different from any she'd experienced before. 'It's very beautiful,' she said quietly. 'But it must have been so very lonely for you with only Rumplestiltskin for company.'

'Yes, it was lonely,' Toby said. 'But it was good to be free. To not have to hide for several days a month and to not have to lie to people. They would have killed me, I'm sure of it, had the curse not come.'

'I don't understand how anyone who heard your howl could hunt you. I found it beautiful.' Petra blushed slightly.

'I'll never forget the first time I heard you howl back to me. It was like seeing a light in the darkness.' Toby said. 'When you called to me from the castle, I knew I had to find you. And I knew when I saw the soldier with his knife at your throat that I had to save you.' He stopped walking and looked at her. 'I'd happily die to save you.'

She smiled at him, warmth rushing through her body.

The howl beyond the forest wall had drawn her to it, and this was why. Toby leaned forward and kissed her and for a moment after his lips left hers she was breathless with the rightness of it all.

'I thought the prince was a fool with his love for Beauty,' she whispered. 'Do you think this is what he feels?' She slid her arms around Toby's waist and rested her head on his chest as he held her. His laughter vibrated through his shirt.

'No, you can't blame the prince for his stupidity. He kissed her and that was his downfall. The water witches are famous for their allure. Their sisters, who live in the Eastern Seas, are called Sirens. They lure men to their deaths on the rocks because the sailors can't resist getting closer to them. Your prince may be a fool in many ways – I can't judge him on that – but where our queen is involved, it is hard to not love her. Her blood dictates that we do.'

He kissed her forehead and she liked the feel of his stubble against her skin. 'This, however,' he said. 'This is a different kind of magic altogether.'

She didn't need to ask what he meant. She felt it inside her. They were made for each other and were destined to be together. Was that why the wolves had come to her grandmother's house so often? Had her longing for him been what had drawn them?

'You should go back,' Toby said softly. 'I can feel it coming and I would rather change alone.'

In his last sentence she could feel the weight of shame he felt about his curse, the loneliness and dread it brought with it, and as she headed back to the oak tree she vowed that, whatever it took, she would break *that* part of the curse – he would never be lonely again.

He joined them ten minutes later, padded over to Petra, curled up beside her on the floor and rested his heavy head in her lap, one ear cocked as the huntsman and Rumplestiltskin continued to talk.

'I won't do it again,' the old man said. 'Everyone I love is dead. My child is dead. Let the city live with the Beast until we're all dead and rotting behind the forest wall.'

'I don't care about your curses or your Beast,' the huntsman countered. 'My responsibility is towards the prince. We cut our way in through the forest, and we can get out again the same way. We don't belong here, it will let us pass. But I need to get to the castle and force him to come with me, and do it without the first minister seeing me. Once we've gone you can do what you like. Hide and die in here, or destroy the spindle and free the city.'

'I will never release them while she lives.'

'Then you should do what you promised your friend the king you would do,' Petra said softly. 'Prick her finger again.'

'And wait another hundred years alone?' Rumplestiltskin's voice trembled with horror at the thought. 'A hundred years, only for someone like you to come along and ruin it again?' He shook his head. 'I could not. I could not. No good comes from curses.'

Petra stroked the wolf's head and thought that Toby should have been dead for decades before she was born. 'Sometimes it can,' she said.

'Just tell me how I can get to the prince without being seen,' the huntsman said. 'I have no loyalty to your first minister and I have no desire to see you dead. But I do have to see the prince and if you can't give me another way in then I'll have no choice but to walk through the castle doors, and then he'll want to know whether I found you. If what you say about the dungeons is true then I will have no choice but to tell him.'

'This isn't my only hiding place,' Rumplestiltskin said roughly, but the huntsman's words had clearly caused him alarm. 'But I will give you a way in. Our tunnels go everywhere.' His untrusting eyes flashed darkly. 'But I will go with you, to be sure you don't betray me. And I will not bring the spindle.'

The network of tunnels that Rumplestiltskin had built was extraordinary, and even with his natural sense of direction and eye for remembering details of a path, the huntsman knew that he would never find his way back without the old man. They'd left Petra sleeping and the wolf had slunk out, no doubt to feed on nearby chickens or other domestic animals.

He pitied the cursed man, wondering how terrible a thing it must be to spend part of your life trapped in an animal's body with all the cravings that came with it. He made a quiet vow to himself never to cross a witch if he could avoid it.

They eventually came up into the dark castle through a fireplace in what appeared to be an empty set of apartments. Rumplestiltskin lowered the hatch back down and stretched as he straightened up.

'How did you know it would be empty?' the huntsman asked, his hand on the hilt of his knife.

'These are my apartments. I doubt anyone is keen to take a traitor's rooms just yet.' It was the dead of night and the castle, the tension eased now that the Beast had left them for a while, slept soundly. They crept through it undisturbed. Under the prince's door, however, a strip of light shone out.

He almost shrieked when he saw them, leaping from his bed and grabbing at an ornament to use it as a weapon. The huntsman rushed over to quieten him as Rumplestiltskin secured the door.

'What did we do?' the prince said, trembling. 'We should never have woken her. We should never have touched her.' He gripped the huntsman's arm. 'I can't get rid of the *taste* of it.'

'You've met the Beast then,' Rumplestiltskin said and the prince shuddered again.

'We need to put everything back as it was,' he said quietly. 'We need to put them all back to sleep.'

'Forget about that,' the huntsman said. 'That's not our business. We need to escape. Cut through the forest as we did before and return to your father.'

'I can't forget it. You didn't see. You didn't see what she did to that serving girl.' The prince frowned slightly and his pale face turned to the huntsman. 'I'll never be able to forget. Not while she's awake.' He paused in his mutterings. 'You *knew* her. That's what he said. He brought her because she'd been talking to you. And then she... and then she...'

'Nell?' the huntsman's blood cooled. 'What did she do to Nell?' The prince's mouth opened as he worked to force out some words, and then he simply burst into tears.

'Blood,' Rumplestiltskin said, quietly. 'She'd have taken her blood. The Beast has a blood lust and the orphaned servants feed it. When the lust is satisfied, the Beast often leaves. It's a price the kingdom must pay.'

'Beauty killed her?' The huntsman was stunned. Even after hearing Rumplestiltskin's tale he found it hard to equate the pretty, kind queen with cruelty. And Nell? She killed Nell?

'She danced in her blood,' the prince moaned. 'She made me... she made me drink it with her. I couldn't stop her. I couldn't...' He looked from one man to the other. 'I was too scared. Can't you see? Can't you understand? I couldn't do anything.' He stared into space. 'She was so beautiful when she was sleeping. How could we have known?'

The horror of his words hung in the air.

'And you want to let her live?' the huntsman rounded on Rumplestiltskin as he thought of poor Nell. The feel of her soft skin and the sound of her easy warm laugh were fresh to him. She had been a sweet girl who'd done nothing wrong and he loathed himself for falling prey to his nature and taking his pleasure with her – especially when he had inadvertently drawn her towards her death. His anger raged. 'Then you let her live. But give me the spindle. You go with the others and cut through the forest. I'll stay behind and curse her again.' He gritted his teeth knowing what he was subjecting himself to. A hundred long years alone. But if it wasn't for him Nell would still be alive. If they hadn't woken Beauty then she would have been sleeping peacefully, her whole life waiting for her when the Beast was dead. He would do it. He had to do it.

'No,' Rumplestiltskin said. 'Why should I? No one cares that my daughter spent her life trapped in that witch's tower. No one cares that I will never look on her face again. So what do I care of the fate of the city?'

'What if you could have another child?' the prince blurted out. There was a mania in his eyes and the huntsman knew that if Beauty wasn't returned to her long dying sleep then the prince would never feel free of her. His terror would drive him mad; if it hadn't a little already. The young man had endured far more adventure than he'd bargained for.

'My wife is dead,' Rumplestiltskin spat bitterly. 'I will not take another.'

'I will give you my child. My first born.' He grabbed the man's arm, his whole body trembling.

'What?' The huntsman turned, his anger over Nell's death sideswiped by shock. 'You can't make a deal like that!'

'I can.' The prince didn't take his eyes from Rumplestiltskin. 'My first child. I promise you. You shall have the first child from my marriage bed to raise as your own.'

'A child?' Rumplestiltskin sat on the edge of the bed and stared at the fireplace. 'A child to raise as my own. Away from court. Away from the games of others. A child to love and never leave.'

'Yes!' the prince nodded, enthusiastically. 'Yes! You have my word.'

'Don't do this,' the huntsman growled. 'This kind of deal is worse than a witch's curse.'

'I have your word?' Rumplestiltskin reached out his hand to the fevered prince.

'You do.'

The two men shook and the deal was done. Watching them, aghast, the huntsman wondered how much madness could be held in one kingdom. Suddenly a hundred years alone did not seem too terrible a fate to be waiting for him.

'Let's go,' the prince said. 'The huntsman can come back

with the spindle while we're cutting through the forest. We could be gone by morning.'

'No,' the huntsman gritted his teeth and tried his best to ignore the prince's indifference to his sacrifice of a hundred years. 'The castle will be waking soon and there won't be enough time. If you're not here then the first minister will know we're escaping and the forest wall will have soldiers along every inch. You have to stay here and act normally. Plan the wedding. Lull them into thinking all is well. Tell them you want another party to celebrate your bride. Make sure all the ministers – and Beauty – drink heavily. Tell her she must sleep well before the wedding and make sure she's in bed by midnight. We will meet you back here and you will leave. I'll give you four hours from then. If you haven't cut through the forest wall, then you will be trapped in slumber with the rest of the city until she is dead.'

'But I can't!' The prince looked horrified. 'How can I pretend everything is fine? With her? How? Surely the ministers will be suspicious?'

'The mind is capable of many things,' Rumplestiltskin said, 'when exposed to true horror. It will protect itself. You should put the day's events down to a dream. A nightmare. They will think you have chosen to forget.'

'I don't know—'

'You have to,' the huntsman snapped. He was tired of the prince's weakness. He was tired of these royals who wrecked ordinary people's lives. 'It's the only way.'

Finally, the prince nodded and straightened up. 'I'll do it.'

He made it sound like a noble sacrifice in the way that only a prince could when surrounded by the sacrifices of others on his behalf.

'Good,' the huntsman said, and nodded to Rumplestiltskin. 'Let's go.'

'I will hold you to your promise, young prince,' the old man said. 'First, I will go to the witch, and then I will come to you. Do not forget me.'

'You have my word,' the prince repeated.

When Petra woke, a small streak of light was cutting through the earthy ceiling. Rumplestiltskin was asleep in the chair and the huntsman had made a place for himself on the floor. There was no sign of the prince. Of Toby. Not wanting to wake them, she crept quietly along the narrow tunnel and up the ladder into the fresh air.

Toby was sitting under a tree in the morning sunshine and he smiled at her. 'They still asleep?'

'Like babies.'

'What a beautiful day.' She sat beside him, the grass dry even though it was only just past dawn. 'Warm too.' He was staring out at the slowly waking city and Petra thought she'd never seen anyone more handsome in her whole life, and nor was she likely to. She reached up and turned his face to hers and slowly kissed him. Despite the stubble on his face his lips were soft as they met hers, his tongue and hers entwining until the heat inside her was too much and she fell backwards, pulling him with her. She slid her hands under his shirt and felt him quiver as she traced her fingers over his flat stomach, teasing the line of hair that ran down from his chest to beyond his belly button.

He groaned and wrapped one hand firmly in her hair as her own moved lower, her breath coming harder as he pushed up her dress. She reached for him through his trousers and he paused and gripped her wrist. His face was flushed and the yellow flecks in his green eyes had brightened with his lust.

'Are you sure?'

She answered by smiling and wrapping her legs around his hips, pulling him towards her.

'I'll take that as a yes,' he managed, before their passion overwhelmed them and any words were lost in mouths and hands and movement and love.

When they were done, they lay together and looked at the sky and laughed and smiled in the way new lovers do, and then kissed some more. Soldiers could have stood over them and Petra wouldn't have noticed. This was true love. She'd realised it the first time she'd seen him, and her heart had known it the first time she'd heard his distant howl through the forest wall. He was for her, and she was for him. Petra and Toby. Petra and the wolf.

'Are you hungry?' he said eventually, gently pushing loose strands of hair out of her face. 'There's a bakery just down there. We could get some bread.'

'What about the first minister's men?' she asked.

'They're not looking for us, they're looking for Rumplestiltskin.' He grinned and got up before pulling her to her feet. 'And if he's not carrying a spindle I doubt very much they'd recognise him. Soldiers, as a rule, aren't the brightest boys. Not in this kingdom at any rate.'

'Then let's get some bread.' She linked her arm through his and they strolled down the path in the sunshine as if they had no cares in the world.

As soon as the waft of baking hit the light breeze, Petra realised just how hungry she was, and they joined the small crowd of early risers waiting for their turn at the baker's hatch. She was lost in her own thoughts of love and laughter, leaning her body into him, needing as much contact as possible, until she felt Toby's grip tighten slightly on her arm, and then the words of those around them became more than just background hubbub and her appetite vanished.

'I just saw the blacksmith's wife. It came into their house through the back door last night. The blacksmith came down to catch it ripping a haunch of venison they'd been saving apart. He said he'd never seen such a beast. Its eyes glowed, that's what the blacksmith said.'

'It's not natural, everyone knows that. All that blue fur. And twice the size of a normal wolf.'

'Should be hunted down. Maybe then the forest will open up.'

'Maybe the wolf's what's cursed us.'

Toby mumbled at the baker who presented him with four large freshly baked rolls, and then he tugged Petra away.

'We'll go to the queen and she'll send soldiers to find it. Nowhere to hide with the forest closed round us. They'll hack it to death. Before it starts coming for the children.'

She kept her arm in his and kept their pace slow as they walked back up the path and the voices faded behind them. Their sentiment echoed loudly in the silence though, Toby's jaw stayed tight and all smiles were gone.

'Don't listen to them,' Petra said. 'They're just stupid gossips.'

'I would never attack children,' he said, through gritted teeth.

'I know,' Petra said. 'Forget about them.' It was easier said than done, and she knew it. 'Come on, let's see if the others are awake. Find out where the prince has gone.'

Beautiful as the day was, she couldn't help but feel a wave of relief when they were underground again. Whatever she'd said to try and make him feel better, Toby was right to worry. Petra might know very little about court life, but she understood village gossips. It didn't take much for a few exaggerated words to become blazing torches and pitchforks, and the idea of a mob coming for Toby made her stomach lurch up to her heart and vice versa.

'No,' Toby said, when they'd heard the huntsman's plan. 'You don't have to do that.'

'Yes, I do.' The huntsman glowered up back from beneath his dark hair. 'That girl's dead because I bandaged Beauty's finger and woke her. I have to put it right.'

'It has to be put right, yes. But not by you.'

Most of the bread lay half-eaten on their plates, any hunger forgotten after hearing of what the Beast had done, and of the prince's deal with Rumplestiltskin. Petra felt quite sick. But nothing could prepare her for what came next.

'I'll do it.' Toby said simply. 'You can all go back to the forest and I'll stay.'

'No,' Petra gasped. 'That's stupid. You have to come too.'

'Why?' He looked at her, his eyes flashing bitterly. 'You've heard what they said. Why would it be different anywhere else? Wherever I go, I'll be hunted. At least here I'll be free.'

'You can't!' Tears sprung to Petra's eyes. 'We can't be apart. I won't leave you!'

'You're better off without me,' he said. 'Safer too. When the mob comes, which they eventually will, they won't take kindly to anyone who's protected me.'

'You can't do it anyway,' the huntsman sighed. 'It must happen tonight. You'll be a wolf.'

'Wait until the morning,' Toby said. 'I can do it then.'

Petra stared at him. The idea of living without him – of knowing that he was just the other side of the wall, living on, young and healthy, as she grew old and died with only the sound of his distant howling drifting through the wood to haunt her – was too much to bear. For a moment she couldn't breathe.

'We can't wait until morning,' Rumplestiltskin said. 'It will be too dangerous; the Beast will be too alert. The plan is set for tonight.'

Petra's head spun. She could see Toby's distress. He didn't want to leave her, but neither did he want to spend his life as an outcast. Always lying to people. Always hiding.

'Wait,' she said, suddenly. 'Wait.' As the perfect thought struck her, she smiled. 'The curse doesn't affect the one who wields it?'

Rumplestiltskin nodded.

'Then I'll do it,' she said. 'Toby can guard the room and I'll prick her finger.'

11

🌢

'I give you this magic...'

The prince was surprised that after the huntsman and Rumplestiltskin had left he did manage to fall asleep for a fitful few hours although he had left all the lamps burning. He met Beauty on the terrace for breakfast and she rose from her chair and dashed towards him, a sweet smile making her face glow.

'I missed you,' she whispered, reaching up on her tiptoes to kiss him. She tasted of the sweet apple she'd been eating, but still his stomach flipped and churned as their lips touched. He focused on the darkness of her hair, so different to the blood-streaked blonde of the Beast who'd tormented him the previous day. He forced the memory away, doing his best to lock it in a far corner of his mind

'I missed you too,' he answered weakly. 'I barely slept.'

The last part wasn't a lie. He wondered if she had realised an entire day was missing from her memory. She took his hand and they sat in the sunshine and she talked merrily about their wedding plans as he forced a pastry and some juice inside him. In the bright daylight, and in the presence of her gentleness, it was almost possible to think that all that had happened had been with someone else completely. The girl was good natured and lovely. She didn't even sound the same as the other.

'And how are you both this morning?'

The prince turned to see the first minister standing in the shadow of the awning.

'Wonderful, thank you,' Beauty answered, gracing him with an affectionate smile. 'And what a glorious day.'

'Just the man,' the prince said, happy to hear how confident his voice sounded. He may have had a moment of weakness when he failed to defend the servant girl – he knew from the huntsman's expression that he thought him a coward – but he was brave. How could the huntsman know what it had been like in there? Would he have behaved any differently? Probably not. The prince could be brave. And he would play his part well today. 'I wanted to have a private dinner tonight. Just Beauty and all her ministers. I'd like to get to know them better – and for them to get to know me – before we have our wedding.' He smiled at Beauty. 'I don't want them to worry that perhaps she's made a bad choice.'

'What a lovely idea,' Beauty exclaimed. 'But how could they think that?'

The prince stood up and went to kiss her. 'I would like to make sure. I want you to be proud of me.'

She wrapped her arms round his neck and laughed and then he spun her off the ground and kissed her. More passionately this time. It was strange this allure she had. He ached for her beauty even as he was revolted by the knowledge of the dormant woman who shared her body.

'This shirt is too hot,' he said. 'I need to change. Shall I meet you by the maze?' he asked her. 'We could walk and make our plans together.'

She nodded, her face shining with love, and he turned away. The first minister followed him back into the castle, his face thoughtful.

'How are you feeling this morning, your highness?'

'Oh, I'm fine.' The prince smiled. 'Tired but fine. I had some terrible dreams. I think I might have had a fever. Or too much wine. And that terrible storm raged all night.' He shuddered as memories of blood and the Beast and the knife rose up unwelcome. 'But now the sun is shining and all is well.'

He knew he wasn't looking entirely normal. He could feel himself trembling and there was an entirely surreal quality to the day, as if perhaps this was the dream and all the horrors he'd experienced were the reality that was waiting for him to wake. But perhaps that would help the first minister to believe him.

'Dreams can be strange things,' the first minister said reassuringly. 'I find it best to keep busy and then they fade quickly.'

'Exactly,' the prince flashed him a smile. 'So will you organise the dinner?'

'Certainly,' he said. 'Hopefully your friends will have returned to us by then.'

'My huntsman is thorough,' the prince said, balling his hands into fists to stop them trembling. 'He will return when he has your traitor and not before. Unless your soldiers find him first, of course.'

'Of course,' the first minister agreed.

'And then we can all live happily ever after.'

The prince had never been so happy to close a door behind him. This was going to be a long day.

He did, in part, take the first minister's advice and kept busy. His stomach was in a knot that somehow the huntsman's and Rumplestiltskin's plan would be found out, and then the full wrath of both queen and ministers would land on him. He wasn't afraid of the dungeons, although he was sure that were he dragged there that would change, but he was afraid of anything that might bring the Beast back.

As he walked through the maze with Beauty, pretending to be enthused about finding the right path through it and laughing loudly when they found themselves in yet another dead end, he fought back images of the writhing couples and the extraordinary pleasure he'd felt before the horrors of the serving girl's death. How could Beauty have wrought it all?

Finally, they found the centre of the maze, a circular space with a waterfall and a stone bench decorated with woodland creatures, and Beauty pulled him towards her and kissed him again, and despite his inner torment he felt himself responding to her. He remembered the full curves of her firm body under the sheer dress the Beast had worn and he felt a sudden urge to rip her clothes from her and take her rough and fast over the bench.

'I can't wait until our wedding night,' she said, softly, her own eyes glazed with longing. 'When at last we can love each other properly.'

A part of his heart broke then. He couldn't help it. He had thought she was so perfect – and, here in the maze, she *was* so perfect – that he wondered if he was still, after everything, a little in love with her. That thought revolted him and instantly all he could see behind his eyes was blood, and the heat of the sun was the feel of it on his skin, and the rush of the waterfall was the sound of her mad laughter as she revelled in death, but still he wanted her. Was that her magic at work, he wondered? How could he tell? If he ever loved a princess again, he decided as they finally strolled back out and towards the castle, he would make sure she was as beautiful on the inside as out before he kissed her. Whatever spell Beauty held over him would soon be over, he comforted himself with that. And when he was gone from here, he would think of her and the Beast no more.

Dinner finally came around and the prince was the perfect host, ensuring everyone's glasses were constantly full and regaling them with tales of his life back at his father's castle. He took time to question all the ministers about their families and their roles in the queen's cabinet and they in turn, as the wine flowed, told him tales of their city that clearly filled them with pride. In the main, he was surprised to realise, they were good men. How much did they love Beauty that they could cope with the Beast? Or were they simply too afraid of her to act? Once again, he felt proud of his own bravery and vital role in the plan to return them to the safety of their slumber. He sipped his wine, careful not to drink too much, and reflected on the huntsman. It was good that he would stay behind and put her back to sleep; that would ensure that when the prince returned home he could tell the story as he wished, with whatever small adjustments were required. This was his adventure; it would be told his way.

'Goodnight, my love,' the prince said, about to leave a swaying and giggly Beauty at her bedroom door. 'Until tomorrow. Until our wedding day.'

Even though his sane mind was desperate to get away from both her and the castle, his heart ached with the knowledge that if all went well, he would never see her face again.

'I love you so much,' she said, squeezing him tightly. 'Tonight, I will go to sleep the happiest girl in the world knowing that you are to be my husband. I'll be dreaming of you and our happiness until I wake, of how perfect our life will be together.'

He was glad her face was pressed against his chest, because although the prince could be weak and selfish and part of his mind and heart had been more damaged than he could yet imagine by his experiences with the Beast, he did not consider himself a cruel man. The knowledge that he was sending her to her death ached inside him in the echo of her happiness. He did care for her – for this sweet girl – how could anyone not? He felt every one of his flaws like knives in his skin, and for a moment she was only Beauty; there was no Beast.

'Dream of us forever,' he whispered. 'And may your dreams be wonderful.'

'Oh, they will be,' she said, squeezing him tighter. 'My sleep will be wonderful because tomorrow we wed.'

When the prince finally walked away, he did not look back. He couldn't bring himself to, and then there was the click of a handle turning and she was gone.

* * *

'So, you're not staying?' he said, slightly dismayed, when he heard the new plan. They'd arrived together an hour or so after the prince had returned to his room, the wolf – a part of the story that the prince felt he could wait until later to hear about – guarding the room outside while they fetched him. He'd changed back into the clothes he'd arrived in, his royal cloak freshly cleaned, and bundled towels arranged under his sheets to look like someone was sleeping there. With the arrangements made and his things gathered and ready to go, a little of his confidence had returned.

'It's better this way,' Petra said. 'And he knows the forest and the forest knows him. If anyone has a chance of cutting you out, it's the huntsman.'

'Yes,' the prince said. 'Yes, I suppose it is.' He smiled at the huntsman. 'It will be good to return together.' In many ways, on reflection, it would be. The prince wasn't entirely sure he could find his way through the forest on his own, and he'd had enough adventures for a lifetime. As for how the story was relayed to the king, he doubted the huntsman would care. He was a rough sort, but he wasn't stupid. He'd know not to contradict the prince. 'And I shall make sure you are rewarded for your noble offer anyway,' he finished.

The huntsman simply nodded, but the prince shook the slight away. They were leaving and that was all that mattered.

'Do you want to stand here all night talking about it, or

shall we get on?' Petra asked. The huntsman grabbed her arm, as she turned towards the door.

'I'm still not happy about this,' he said.

'Well, I am.' She smiled and her elfin face was transformed into something beautiful. 'We'll have a hundred years together, and then after that we'll get to grow old. What other lovers have had that opportunity?'

Rumplestiltskin was carefully pulling the spindle from his knapsack and the girl looked at him with a strange affection as she opened the bedroom door and led them back out into the corridor, the wolf immediately rubbing itself against her leg. She stepped closer to the huntsman so the old man was out of earshot. 'When you get back to the forest, tell him he must go to my grandmother's house and tell her his story. '

'Why?'

'Just make sure he does. It's important. Also, have him tell her to listen for me at the forest wall.' She reached up and kissed the huntsman on the cheek, and then did the same to the prince before taking the spindle from Rumplestiltskin. 'Now go.'

'I give you this magic,' Rumplestiltskin said. 'I hope it brings you better luck than it did me.'

Petra smiled at the old man. 'It will. And we'll make sure it works this time.'

'Good luck.' The prince said, his feet itching to be gone.

Every second they loitered was another moment they could be caught.

'Three hours, remember,' Petra said. She smiled once more, and then with her red cloak flowing behind her and the blue wolf leading her, she turned and ran down the corridor towards the queen's apartments.

12

'*See to the queen!*'

The forest wall was battling them every inch of the way as the three men hacked and squeezed their way through the branches and vines, repeating the method the huntsman, Petra and the prince had used, holding a small space open while they cut through to the next. None spoke as they worked, all three aware that they weren't going fast enough. The forest had been tough before but this time the branches seemed aggressive. Even before they'd travelled the first foot, the prince's shirt had been torn, leaving a small piece of cloth flapping on a thorn behind them.

The enchanted kingdom was still visible through the gaps and they must have been working at it for more than an hour. Even in the dead of night it was hot, sweaty work and they gasped and cursed quietly with every tiny step forward.

'Will we make it?' the prince asked, breathless.

'Maybe,' the huntsman grunted, hacking at a thick branch with his small axe. 'Maybe not. If we wake up in a hundred years with trees growing out of our arses, then I'd say we didn't make it.'

'*Hey!*'

Light from a flaming torch swept over them, and a horse whinnied as the patrol came to a halt.

'*Sir, look! There's someone cutting through the wall!*'

The light pressed against the branches and for a second the three men froze, but it didn't help. They'd been seen.

'*It's him! Rumplestiltskin! Get after him!*'

'*You! Get back to the castle! Quickly! Tell the ministers!*'

Suddenly, the greenery behind them was being vigorously attacked by swords and a group of soldiers was following them into the wall.

The huntsman beat at the wood faster, painfully aware that there was only three or four feet between them and that the soldiers would be stronger.

'Come on, come on,' the prince muttered, pressing his weight against the resistant hedge so the huntsman could move further.

'I'm doing my best,' the huntsman growled.

'*I can see them. The bastards! I can see them!*'

There was a flash of steel as the men behind them lunged

forwards, thrusting their blades through the gaps.

The prince cried out as the tip of a sword slashed into his side.

The huntsman found he could work quicker after that.

Petra had pulled a chair close to the queen's bed, and with the wolf beside her, occasionally licking her hand, she'd held the spindle on her lap and watched Beauty sleep as the quiet minutes passed. The prince had done his job well and she was dead to the world. The phrase hurt Petra's heart with the truth in it. If everything went according to plan, she'd never wake again.

She couldn't help but feel sorry for her. Despite the Beast who resided inside her she was the sweetest of girls and, water witch magic or not, Petra felt a pull towards her. The terrible things that were her nature were also not her fault. Petra imagined that if Beauty knew the suffering she'd inflicted on her subjects, or what she'd done to her poor father, she would prick her finger herself. Still, lying there so still, she looked perfect.

Petra wondered how many more hours in the decades to come she would sit in this chair and wonder about the girl who would sleep until her last drop of blood had fallen. She ran her fingers through the wolf's rough fur, taking comfort from the heat of his head.

Suddenly, the wolf's ears pricked up and he let out a low growl. All thoughts of the queen's tragic life vanished as Petra sat up straight, her nerves jangling.

'What is it, Toby?' she whispered, but within a second she had her answer. There was movement in the corridors. From outside, the sound of people urgently calling to each other drifted up to them. Despite the urge to get up and look, Petra stayed by the bed, her hand hovering over Beauty's delicate, pale fingers. Her heart raced as the noise in the corridors grew louder, footsteps dashing this way and that, and men barking commands.

Her heart raced, and the wolf's hackles rose, his fur puffing out so much that he truly looked like a magnificent unnatural beast. She needed to give the huntsman and Rumplestiltskin the longest time possible to get away. They did not deserve a hundred years' sleep, or to wake to find everyone they loved lost. And her grandmother did not deserve to die without knowing Petra's choice or meeting Rumplestiltskin. She gritted her teeth. She was ready to do it, but not until the very last minute.

As the noise grew around them, Beauty stirred but she did not wake. The wolf was ready to pounce and pin her down should she try and run, but Petra hoped beyond hope it wouldn't come to that. What if the Beast woke when she was terrified? What would happen to them all then?

'The prince is gone!' a voice shouted. *'He's tricked us!'*

'See to the queen! Check her majesty is safe!'

Petra was staring so fixedly at the main doors to the queen's bedroom that the secret side entrance, hidden in a panel in the wall next to the wardrobe, slid open and the first minister was inside before she could react. She almost dropped the spindle in surprise and with a growl, the wolf prepared to spring.

For a moment, amidst all the commotion outside, the old man said nothing. He stared at Petra and the spindle and then at the girl in the bed.

'Stay quiet,' he said and then strode to the doors.

Petra's mind was racing and she kept one hand firmly on the wolf who she could feel was ready to spring and rip the minister's throat out to protect her. She still had time to do it. Even if he screamed blue murder into the corridor. There was no need for more bloodshed than necessary but the wolf, although still Toby, thought in more black and white terms than that.

The first minister opened the door a fraction. 'Her majesty is sleeping. She's fine,' he said quietly. 'Now find that prince!'

He closed the door again and leant against it. For a long moment he stared at Petra and she saw the conflict in his face, and then the tired sadness that he carried for his own complicity with the Beast.

'They will come back,' he said quietly. 'And she will wake.

The Beast will sense the trouble.' He walked over to the window and stared out at the peaceful kingdom for a moment, before sitting down on the window seat with a heavy sigh.

'If you're going to do it,' he stretched his legs out and leant his head back on the soft cushions, 'then do it now.'

Petra looked out at the sky that was streaking with purple dawn and hoped that she'd given them enough time, and then, with a deep breath, she carefully lifted the girl's slim forefinger and jabbed the sharp spindle into it.

The huntsman and Rumplestiltskin pulled the bleeding prince through the last of the branches just as the air around them trembled and a wave of heat rushed through the tightening branches, filling the air with the scent of a thousand types of bark and leaf and flower. The wall shimmered momentarily and sparkled in the breaking dawn.

The three men stared as they panted, the prince hunched over slightly as his side bled. If they had thought the wall was dense before, it was now completely impenetrable.

'Well, that answers that then,' the huntsman said, nodding at the men who had been so close behind them. The soldiers had fallen instantly asleep and, held up by the branches, vines were now curling up around their limbs. After a few seconds they were no longer visible.

They all stared at the wall as the relief of their freedom

sank in, along with the exhaustion in their limbs.

'I want to go home,' the prince said, weakly.

Rumplestiltskin looked around him, scanning the horizon for something familiar.

'What now for you?' the huntsman asked.

'The tower.' There was no hesitation. 'I will have my revenge on that witch, and I will see my daughter's grave.' His freedom from the city and the return of Beauty to her sleeping death had not eased his bitterness. He looked at the pale prince, who was examining his flesh wound with more than a touch of horror. 'And then I shall be back to hold you to your word.'

The prince nodded but said nothing.

'There was something else,' the huntsman added, as he slung his bag back over his shoulder and prepared to move on. 'Something Petra made me promise to tell you. She said it was important. About visiting her grandmother...'

Dawn claimed the silent city as the first drop of blood hit the floor beside the sleeping Beauty's bed. In the glass by her bed, the rose drooped ever so slightly. Petra gave Beauty one last look and then went out into the corridor to join Toby who smiled at her and her heart sang.

'No more wolf for a month,' he said.

'Shame,' she said, taking his arm. 'He's a good-looking

creature. I guess I'll have to make do with you at night until then.' They stepped carefully over the sleeping bodies and their shoes tapped out against the marble, the only feet that would walk these corridors for a long, long time. 'Let's get some breakfast. I'm starving.'

'Do you think they made it?' Toby asked as they turned onto the sweeping staircase.

'I think so,' she answered. 'This adventure deserves a happy ending.' She rested her head on his arm. 'Other than ours.'

'What was all that about your grandmother?' he asked. 'And Rumplestiltskin.'

Her smile stretched wider as she thought of how happy those two would be when they met. 'I couldn't tell him. I don't think he'd have let me stay here if I had. My great-grandmother made me this cloak, you know. Well, she made it for my grandmother. She said it was her favourite colour because it reminded her of her father.'

'I'm not following,' Toby said. 'What's that got to do with Rumplestiltskin?'

'She was a strange woman,' Petra said. 'She arrived in the village out of nowhere when she was twenty-two. When my grandmother was little she told her stories of her childhood, of being trapped in a tower by a witch until one day a handsome prince rescued her.' She paused. 'It clearly didn't work out, but she left my grandmother and then my mother and then me, with a healthy cynicism about Prince Charmings that stuck, even though we never really believed her stories.'

Toby turned and stared at her. 'You think your great-grandmother was Rumplestiltskin's daughter?' Sunlight burst through the castle windows and

Petra knew it was going to be a beautiful day. 'Her name was Rapunzel,' she said. 'So yes, I think she was.'

EPILOGUE

'You stay here,' the huntsman said, after carefully bandaging the prince's wound and setting a fire. 'We'll make camp for the night and then tomorrow we'll figure out where we are.'

Somehow, and he wondered if it was the forest's wiles at work, they had lost their bearings and even the huntsman thought they might have strayed into a separate kingdom rather than the prince's own. Still, what more could happen to them? They'd have a good rest and then they'd be on their way. The prince's wound would not kill him and a few extra days in the forest would do neither of them any harm.

'Don't be too long,' the prince said, a sorry sight with his royal cape wrapped round him and his face pale and sweating. 'I don't want to be alone. I keep thinking about her. About Beauty.' The huntsman slapped him gently on his shoulder.

'These woods are rich. There'll be food aplenty and I'll be back soon enough.' He picked up his bag and carried it with him, even though he only needed his knife. He'd earned the diamond shoes, but if the prince found them he would have to give them up, and something raw and animal in his soul told him that he could not let that happen.

He left the prince staring into the fire torn between grief and celebration – Beauty and the Beast – and headed out of the clearing.

It was a warm day in the forest and even though it made the hair on his chest tickle with sweat as he moved through the trees, that pleased the huntsman. Heat slowed animals as much as men and although his skills were such he had no doubt meat would roast over the fire tonight, the task was going to be easier than expected. He could counter the laziness that came with the sun and force himself to be alert. It was unlikely to be the same for the animals in this dense woodland. So far, apart from an old crone scurrying between the trees just before he'd spied the stag, he'd seen little sign of human habitation and he'd heard no horn blowing for a Royal hunt. It was wild here. He liked that...

THE END

The end... or is it just the beginning?

High in her tower the clever witch smiled,
the spindles around her so many beguiled.

How easy it was to riddle with men,
and now Beauty was deep in her death-sleep again.

The princess was cursed, both without and within,
Yet one thing could save her: a love free from sin.

The Kingdoms would change; there would be war
     and fear,
And Beauty would sleep for a full hundred years,

What happened then was a mystery, she knew,
But she had great faith in kisses that were true...

ABOUT THE AUTHOR

Sarah Pinborough is a critically acclaimed horror, thriller and YA author. She has written for *New Tricks* on the BBC and has an original horror film in development. Sarah won the British Fantasy Award for Best Novella with *Beauty* in 2013, Best Short Story in 2009, and has three times been short-listed for Best Novel. She has also been short-listed for a World Fantasy Award.

www.sarahpinborough.com

For more fantastic fiction, author events, exclusive
excerpts, competitions, limited editions and more

VISIT OUR WEBSITE
titanbooks.com

LIKE US ON FACEBOOK
facebook.com/titanbooks

FOLLOW US ON TWITTER
@TitanBooks

EMAIL US
readerfeedback@titanemail.com